Ensnared by the Shadow King

Night's Curse
Book One

Lola Glass

Cover by Claire Holt with Luminescence Covers

https://www.luminescencecovers.com/

To my husband, for loving my inner wolf

BL

ELEMENTAL
QUEENDOMS

SO
PRO

NIGHT
COURT

SAVAGE
DOMAIN

THUNDER
ISLE

HM

SIREN
ISLE

GARGOYLE
RUINS

AR
ICES

LUNAR
ISLE

ICE
KINGDOMS

Chapter 1

My knees kissed the grass, my fingers digging into the cold, wet dirt beneath it. The damp, tangled black strands of my hair brushed the earth next to my knees. Tears stung my eyes as they scanned the dark horizon of a world I'd never dared imagine—all I'd ever known was cracked concrete walls and cold, cruel chains.

"Finally," Akari breathed. She stood beside me, her pale arms spread wide and her face tilted toward the night sky above us. Her white hair, just as wet and wild as mine, fell below her ass with her head leaned back like that.

"Look at the stars," Vena murmured. Unlike me and Akari, she stood with her arms wrapped around her middle, trapping her own ratted, dripping golden hair to her waist. We were all dressed in large, slightly blood-stained men's clothing that belonged to the guards we'd been forced to kill during our escape.

Seeing our world was a relief for Vena and Akari, but it wasn't new to them like it was to me. They'd been raised in the real world, but all I'd ever known was the prison that had held us for nearly twenty-one years. And though Vena and Akari were older than me, we all looked about the same age because fae stopped aging in our mid-twenties.

The scent of the world outside my prison and the feeling of being free were so new to me, so strange, that I almost didn't know whether to embrace them or run.

My fingers dug further into the dirt, or soil, or whatever the hell was beneath me.

No, I wouldn't run.

I was free.

"We need to go," Akari finally said, after a few moments of silence. The wind rustled my hair, blowing against my skin, in a way that only struck me with more awe.

"Ready, Diori?" Vena asked me, her voice quiet.

I couldn't find the words, so I dipped my head in a nod.

Akari's hand slid gently around my bicep, and I stood without assistance despite her soft, unfamiliar grip.

Though we'd spent two decades together, we had never touched. The chains we'd worn hadn't allowed it.

And though I had never been outside my prison, over the last few years, Vena and Akari had told me everything they knew and had seen, so I was somewhat prepared.

Akari released my arm when she was sure I was steady on my feet, and then together, we ran.

BY THE TIME we stopped at an inn, we'd been running for half a day. We were all starving, but hunger wasn't new to us.

Akari pulled a few of the coins (we'd taken them from our captors) out of a pocket on the stolen mens' clothing we all wore, and the three of us ignored every stare sent our way while we dropped into chairs and waited.

Someone brought our food over, and I tried not to stare at the bowl of stew set in front of me. It smelled like nothing I'd ever imagined, so hot it was steaming, and was served in a pretty off-white bowl.

Knowing I was being strange, I forced myself to pick up the spoon, and began eating slowly. I'd used to inhale food like an animal, but Vena and Akari had taught me how to be a person—a woman, in particular.

So I ate at a "normal" pace, despite the pit in my stomach and the other-worldly taste of the stew.

With our hunger sated, we headed up to our room quietly. People had been staring at us, but we didn't care.

Not after what we'd survived.

The inn had a bathroom with running water, which I'd heard about but never experienced. We took turns in the shower, and I kept my shock at the running water to myself as I scrubbed multiple years' worth of dirt off my skin.

After we were all clean, dressed only in the dirty shirts we had stolen from the captors we'd killed, we sat on the single, large bed together. Its softness shocked me, but I kept that shock to myself, as I did most emotions.

"We'll stay for three more days, and purchase clothes and weapons," Akari said, her icy blue eyes meeting Vena's, and then mine. "We'll eat, gather strength, plan... and then, we find the kings who cursed us and get our revenge."

"And our freedom," I murmured.

"And our peace." Vena's voice was barely above a whisper.

Our hands met. For the first time, they were all clean.

The magic that had been forced upon us twenty-one years ago leaked and whirled and grew over our hands and arms where they were physically connected. Mine was the magic of shadows, Akari's was the magic of moonlight, which was called night magic, and Vena's was the magic of an all-consuming darkness.

A yawn escaped me, and my leaking magic vanished.

Our hands separated, our lips lifting slightly as we looked around our group.

We'd done it.

We were alive, and we were free from our chains.

And soon, we'd be free of the curses that had gotten us captured in the first place.

The kings would die...

And we would never be chained again.

CHAPTER 2

FOUR DAYS LATER, I walked away from the inn dressed in a simple black slip dress that fell to my ankles and matched most of the clothing on the other women I passed. A golden dagger was strapped to my thigh, the sheath visible through the dress's slit with every step I took.

In the Night Court, the moon was always up, the stars were always out, and the shadows were always dancing. The wealthy wore white and silver, like the moon, and the poor wore black, with jewelry made from gold because of its low price.

I wasn't ashamed to embrace my lack of status. I had been born to nothing, and made into a monster by the king I now hunted—the man who I would destroy to save myself.

Twenty-one years earlier, I'd been an infant without enough magic to survive on my own, doomed to an early death. Then the Night King had passed away unexpectedly around the time of my birth, without choosing one of his three sons to inherit the throne and the immense power that accompanied it.

The power had split between his kids, but the throne's magic wasn't compatible with the king's sons' personal magic. The three of them were being torn to shreds by the power within them until they found three powerless fae women to take their magic—me, Akari, and Vena. My magic had belonged to the youngest of the king's sons, who was now a king himself.

The shadow magic had both saved my life and ended it in one fell swoop, keeping me alive by giving me the power I needed to survive, but landing me in the hands of those who wanted to use the king's power through me.

Those men and women had trapped my friends and I, locking us in chains that would be burned into our minds, souls, and bodies for the rest of our existence. They'd experimented on us, tortured us, starved us, and anything else they could think of in an attempt to remove the kings' magic from us, but they had never succeeded.

I'd wished for death many times in my two decades of hell, but fae were damned near immortal. We died if we were killed, but murder was an unforgivable sin that would get a person cast out to a hellishly bright island just off the coast of our land. Night fae like us needed moonlight to use our magic; too much sun would drain us until we passed on to the mysterious life that followed this one.

But I would happily accept a life of sunshine and a trip to the next existence if it meant I was free of the demonic shadow magic lying beneath my skin, always waiting to take over and deliver hell to anyone or anything around me.

And considering that I'd been the one to end the lives of the guards holding us captive before Akari, Vena, and I escaped, I was likely already doomed to spend the rest of my time on the bright island.

The inn my friends and I had stayed in was in the Shadow King's portion of our land—and he was the king I needed to kill to be free. My target wasn't the cruelest of the brothers, but he was constantly at war with the Dark King, which didn't exactly bode well for those living in his territory.

It did, however, make me feel slightly better about the fact that I was going to have to kill him.

As I walked, the magic I emanated and the scars on my wrists drew more attention than I liked, but I ignored the stares of the other fae who passed me on the road to the castle. My magic—the king's magic—was strong, and anyone passing me would feel its heartbeat as I passed them, so there was no way around that and therefore no point in fearing it.

And there would be time to worry about what others thought of me on the sunny isle, where I couldn't hurt anyone. If I let myself worry while I walked, there was no telling what my magic might do to those who stared.

The sky remained dark throughout my journey, as it always would so long as the Night King did his job properly. While the moon was up, our people were nearly invincible, which protected us from the other lands of fae, gargoyles, gods, and beasts.

Hours passed, and eventually, I grew tired and decided to stop for the night. There had been enough money left to get my friends and I to our destinations safely, so I found another inn and managed to sleep a few hours. The chains were all I'd ever known, so I didn't have nightmares about them—though there was a phantom ache in my wrists and ankles when I woke.

After a large breakfast, I returned to the road, and continued on my way.

AFTER ANOTHER DAY OF WALKING, and another stop at an inn, I reached the city the next morning. Though we lived in a state of constant night, we still considered our waking hours "days". Our bodies were naturally attuned to the awake and asleep patterns of our days and nights, which was useful.

Awe filled me as I wandered the streets of the city. The streets were full of those selling goods, trying to call attention to themselves and survive in the dark world we called home.

As I walked, my fingers brushed soft, luxurious fabrics, and pulled back at sharp decorative items. I'd showered at the inn and washed my dress in water too, so I wasn't filthy, and I loved the freedom my cleanliness gave me to explore.

As I wandered, a woman caught my wrist.

My magic tensed in my chest, its heartbeat thrumming with mine as I spun to face her.

When I saw that she wore the same simple black fabric as I did, her eyes flashing a bit desperately, I forced myself to breathe steadily.

My magic dissipated slowly as it realized I wasn't in danger, thankfully.

"Bracelets," the woman said, gesturing to a cylindrical rack of golden bands. Most of them at least partially resembled the chains I'd worn on my wrists for so long—the ones I despised with every ounce of my being. "I have bracelets," she continued. "To hide your scars."

I retracted my wrist from her grip rapidly. "Why should I hide the evidence of my survival?"

Her nose wrinkled. "It's an imperfection."

"I far prefer imperfection to lies." After spinning on my heels, I slipped through the crowd, headed toward the castle once again.

No more distractions.

I was there for a purpose.

I wove through the city, ignoring all other calls from those who wanted me to purchase their goods. My coin pouch was tucked into my underclothing, secured against my hip, at the warning of the shopkeeper my friends and I had purchased clothes from. Thieves on the road would take what they could see and reach, he had warned.

Except weapons; few were daft enough to steal a weapon.

And though I didn't know how to use the dagger on my thigh, it was still comforting to have it there.

I reached the castle an hour later, my heart beating a bit quickly as I approached. My magic responded solely to my emotions, so I fought to keep myself calm, to keep the beast within me at bay.

The castle wasn't a monstrosity, like I'd expected it to be after Akari's description of the one she was raised in. The Shadow King's was large and beautiful, but not unbelievably so.

Shaped like a miniature mountain, the castle was built on a foundation of stairs. The building itself was wide on the bottom, and narrowed as it stretched upward, with three peaks at the top.

The walls of the structure were crafted entirely from shiny stone that seemed to have been pumped full of shadow and smoke. The vapor within looked more like it was swaying and dancing the longer my eyes were trained on it.

Shaking my head at the walls, I focused on the doors.

There were no guards outside, protecting the building the way I expected them to be.

Maybe they were inside, with the king.

It didn't matter; I would get past them, wherever they were. If they wanted to kill me, they'd have to go through my magic.

And no one but Vena and Akari survived my magic.

My bare feet padded lightly on the shadowy stairs. The shadows in the stone seemed to gather beneath me, growing darker as my toes and the silk of my dress slid over them.

When I reached the massive double doors, my hand pressed to the surface of the one nearest to me. I almost expected someone or something to come out and attack me, to tell me I didn't belong there, or to somehow sense that I meant to kill the king.

None of that happened, though.

The stone was smooth and warm beneath my palm, and slid open easily when I pushed lightly against it. Something about the castle felt... familiar.

I assumed the magic in its walls was responsible for that feeling, and stepped inside.

My eyes trailed over the large, friendly space. It wasn't empty like my prison had been, or simple like the inns I'd stayed in. The floor was covered in more of the smooth, smokey stone, the ceiling far above my head made entirely of glass, allowing the moon and stars to shine into the space.

Couches and chairs faced one another out in front of me, with a few people sitting in various places on them. Some looked to be practicing magic, while others conversed. They all wore white or silver, making their wealth obvious.

A large staircase stretched upward to my left, and another set of double doors like the ones I'd just come through were off to my right a bit.

"Hello." One of the women on the couch noticed me and waved, catching me off guard. "Can we help you?"

Despite the obvious difference in our financial levels, she didn't sneer at me.

"The king. I'm looking for the king," I managed to say.

"Of course. Just through those doors." She gestured toward the double doors to my right.

I nodded once and then strode toward them. Though I was tense and ready for one of the fae on the couches to realize what I was there to do and attempt to stop me, their conversation resumed, and I may as well have not existed to them at all.

My feet were silent on the stone as I opened the door, slipping into the room.

As soon as I was inside, my gaze slid over the space.

There was a throne off to one side, nestled in the far corner of the room as if it was barely a side-thought. The rest of the space seemed to have been dedicated to training. Weapons of all shapes, colors, and sizes studded the walls, as well as weapon racks and other items I didn't recognize. Beneath my feet, the floor was made of something thick and slightly squishy.

In the center of the room, two men and one woman sparred with swords. The man furthest from me was mostly hidden from my sight by the other two people, but as far as I could see, he had deeply-tanned skin and dark hair; he seemed to be facing off against both the woman and the other man.

The woman had olive skin and shimmering red hair, and had on a simple white slip dress with a skirt that fell to the middle of her thighs with a slit going up to her hip. Her dress billowed out slightly with every rapid twist, spin, and turn she made, flashing the silver undergarment she wore beneath it. Her hair was either short or braided back; I couldn't tell while she moved like that.

The second man was massive and dark-skinned, with long black hair in a thick braid that fell nearly to his waist. It moved as he did, but he didn't spin and twist the way the woman beside him did; his movements were strong, powerful, and determined. He wore only a pair of simple white silk pants that looked to be made out of the same smooth fabric that my dress and most of the clothing in the Night Court was made out of.

My gaze followed their movements for a bit. The way they fought was a dance; the way they reacted and responded to each other's movements a work of art.

I hated to stop them, to cause anyone pain like that which I'd suffered, but there was no other choice. When I discovered which of the men was the king, I'd have to end him. It was the only way to true freedom.

Shadows began to spin through the room, slowly setting to work. My eyes tracked them easily; they were a part of me as much as they were the king.

It only took a moment for me to determine what was happening.

The shadows were slowly sliding off of the man whose appearance was mostly hidden from me by his companions and their rapid battle; and they were working with him. *For* him. Sliding under his companion's feet, making them slip. Blurring the man's movements to confuse them. Slowly making the room darker, distorting their ability to see.

The massive man with the long braid countered the shadow magic with a bit of moonlight that glowed off his sword. Every swing of the weapon cut through the magical shadows, brightening the room and clearing his vision.

Alternatively, the woman in silver seemed to grow darker herself, her skin emanating the deep darkness of that particular brand of our people's magic.

The fight only grew more intense, more shadows filling the room. Despite the light and dark magic that fought them, the shadows only grew thicker and heavier.

My chest seemed to expand as I inhaled the magic. The scent of it allowed me to breathe deeper and heavier than I had in a long time, if ever. The shadows weren't just magic or power to me; they were life.

The life that had earned me the scars on my wrists and the torture in my memories.

My fists clenched at the reminder.

I was free now; I was going to be free.

Eventually, the magic in the room cleared, and I saw both the massive man and the red-haired woman on their backs on the ground. They were each bleeding in multiple places, though I would've seen the wounds slowly knitting back together if I were closer.

And the man who had been fighting them—the King of Shadows—stood grinning down at them in victory.

He wasn't built like a mountain, the way the massive man was, though he was probably the tallest person I'd ever seen. Instead, his shoulders were broad and his waist tapered, every muscle on his body defined and on display. His simple white pants fell to his ankles, leaving hardly anything to the imagination for any woman nearby.

The king tossed his swords to the floor, ignoring their clang as he offered his hands to his companions. They both grudgingly accepted the offer, gripping his hands and allowing him to pull them to their feet.

"That was better," the king told them, nodding his head. "Your magic is flowing more easily."

"Not easily enough," the woman grumbled, wiping dust and blood off her arm with her palm as she tossed her sword to the ground too.

"We have a visitor," the massive man stated, turning toward me.

Then they were *all* looking at me.

And though Vena and Akari had taught me how to speak with people, I wasn't *good* at it.

"What can we do for you?" the woman asked, her voice curt as her hand lifted to her hip. She stepped backward into place beside the king, and the massive man who had been fighting with her followed suit. Though, he didn't look as critical of me as she did.

"I need to speak with the king," I said, hoping my voice came out strong. "Alone."

The woman made a noise of disagreement.

Was she his lover?

Fae took mates, but only if they were fated, as far as I knew. If the woman and the king had been fated, it would've shown on their throats in the words of a forgotten language.

There weren't many mated couples, according to Akari and Vena. But those who were, were inseparable. They were so possessive and protective of each other that most fae hoped never to possess a bond like that.

So most fae took lovers, and held on to each other only if there was no sign of their connection being soul-deep.

I had no feelings on it either way; my only focus was my freedom. Should my friends and I end the lives of the kings without losing our own, we had plans to meet back at that inn we'd spent days in together, precisely one year from the day we left. If we didn't survive, we would mourn one another fiercely.

Should I survive without getting sent to the bright isle and find one of my friends missing on the day we met again, I would do whatever it took to reach the isle myself, to free whoever was lost or remain there with her permanently.

"Out, Lavee. Jesh, make sure she puts something on the leg wound she's ignoring," the king said, slipping his hands into the pockets on his pants.

The woman—Lavee, I assumed—grumbled something about his stubborn ass as she stalked out of the room, walking past me with a warning glare.

The man—Jesh—followed her, nodding politely at me as he passed me.

As the door closed behind them, I focused on my memories and my emotions.

"What do you wish to discuss?" the king's eyes slowly trailed up and down my body as he crossed the room, stopping a few feet in front of me. A few of his shadows slid off his skin a bit, whispering something I couldn't understand, but I forced myself to ignore them.

My eyes closed, and my anger and pain flared. The magic within me bloomed furiously, raging through my chest and middle.

Shadows leaked from my skin as if they could no longer be contained within my body. My control slipped away, and the monster that raged within me took complete control. Shadows consumed my flesh as the power transformed me, changing my figure.

A savage snarl escaped the monster inhabiting my very soul as she flew toward the Shadow King, her teeth bared and ready to tear through his throat.

CHAPTER 3

SURPRISE FLOODED the king's eyes as the monster's teeth clamped down on his throat. I'd seen him in action—I knew he could've reacted—but either surprise or lack of worry had stopped him. He stumbled backward, crashing to the ground with the massive weight of her, but he didn't seem to care. His eyes looked up at her in wonder, of all things.

Though her teeth clamped onto his throat, they didn't cut his skin—they didn't tear his flesh, either. It was as if he was covered in some kind of invisible shield that protected him from the sharpness of her fangs.

His fingers slipped into her fur, and she released his throat.

Confusion flooded the monster.

The moment her rage—and my rage—calmed, the magic rippled over her skin, and sank back into my chest.

I panted hard, glowering down at the king I was now lying on top of. My hand shook as I reached for the knife from the sheath on my thigh, wrestling the infuriatingly-silky fabric away from it.

The king made no move to stop me as I ripped the knife from its sheath and plunged it toward his throat.

The tip of the blade halted a breath against his skin, just like the monster's teeth had.

There were no shadows, no form of night magic blocking my blade.

Confusion and panic had me stabbing the knife downward again, and again, though I saw no results from the motion.

The king's huge hand wrapped around mine. He dragged my knife away from his throat—and then from my grip—and tossed it across the room. His gaze was locked on mine, and he stared at me with wonder as he murmured, "You are absolutely magnificent."

His eyes were a disarming light gray, the shadows within them swirling slowly, but I forced myself not to acknowledge that.

I rolled off his abdomen, scrambling to my feet and staring at him in panic, my mind rushing to try to catch up with everything that had happened.

I'd had him—I'd killed him. Or I would've. But something stopped me—some kind of magic.

"What was that?" I demanded.

"Magic cannot destroy itself." The king sat up, his gaze once again sliding over me, over my body. "Your magic lives in your very veins—the same magic that once lived in mine, and still does in small amounts. You're her. My salvation."

"You're the reason I'm a monster," I snarled back. "Fix this. Take this magic *back* if it won't allow me to end you and it both."

"I can't do that until I've retrieved the rest of the throne's magic from my brothers." His gaze landed back on my face, as if he couldn't stop himself from staring at me, taking me in.

"Then do it," I spat.

"I've been trying to for nearly two decades. All I possess is the court's magic right now, which my brothers also possess—and like yours and mine, it cannot destroy itself." His lips curved upward wickedly. "But now that you're here, with my magic, we'll take the power from them. The throne will be mine, and I'll free you from my shadows."

"I *won't* be your weapon." My fists curled at my sides, my fury bringing the monster in my chest to life again.

This time, I wasn't doing it on purpose.

So this time, I had no sway over her actions.

The magic exploded from my chest, swallowing the castle in shadows as the beast ripped my control away. My heart pounded in my ears like the beat of a drum as the shadowed wolf that took over lunged through the castle.

Like me, she had spent her life in chains.

And like me, she was more desperate for freedom than she could ever explain.

Though shadows darkened the entirety of the castle, she saw with her other senses as she ran from the king, fury and fear coursing through her veins together.

She charged out of the room, finding the fae on the couches blocking her path out. Her teeth shredded the skin of one of them, relishing the scream as the blood coated her tongue.

Another pained cry for help followed, and another, and another.

She wasn't ending their lives, but she was coming close— very, very close.

Plunging through the darkness, she shoved through the castle's doors, ignoring their heavy weight as she fought the magic for escape.

When she broke through, she ran for the forest.

For the closest thing she could get to freedom.

And when anyone got in her way, she made them bleed.

.   .   .

THE MAGIC DISSIPATED as the beast reached the forest, and the shadows faded before dropping me on the forest floor, on my hands and knees. Blood drenched my face and neck, soaking my hair and hands too. There were a few new holes in my dress, and a few wet, bloody spots as well.

My chest heaved as I panted, my head drooping toward the dirt floor that my sticky hair brushed.

Tears burned my eyes as the images of what the monster within me had done to those in the city came back to me. The memories cut through my chest like knives, one, by one, by one.

I hated what I was.

I hated that I couldn't control it.

That I housed this magic so wild, so violent, so...

Branches cracked off to my side, and my head jerked toward the noise.

My magic swelled in my chest again.

"It's just me." The Shadow King lifted his hands up in surrender.

Just him?

The tall, muscular, gorgeous king of the damned court?

"What do you want?" I snarled at him.

He couldn't take my magic, and I couldn't kill him, so what was the point of being there? I needed to find a place far from other living creatures, where I could survive without hurting anyone else.

"You didn't kill anyone, back there. Thought you might want to know that." His hands slipped into his pockets, and he strolled, barefoot, closer to me. The man seemed even bigger, now that we were out in the forest. Despite what had just happened, his shoulders were relaxed and the bottom hem of his pants swayed slightly around his ankles, drawing my attention to the muscular thighs they outlined. "I kept them alive."

My magic swelled within me as he came closer—the threat of him.

Stars, he was huge.

"Stay where you are."

He stopped. "I know how difficult it is to control my magic. The power within you belongs to me—I held it for the first seventeen years of my life. I had to give it to you, to survive my father's death and the court's magic that was transferred to me."

"So what?" I tried to stop snarling, but the beast in me was strong, and angry... and afraid.

"So I can teach you how to control it. Show you the methods I used to keep it at bay, until I've conquered my brothers and can remove most of it from you."

"Most?"

He nodded once. "You were an infant, and you were dying. I suppose you don't remember, but I'll never forget. There wasn't enough magic in your blood to sustain you, then. I'll leave you enough to survive, when I reclaim my power."

I scoffed. "I don't want your magic." Standing up, I brushed my dress off frustratedly. All the movement truly did was smear blood over my hands and more of my dress, but I ignored it. I wasn't exactly new to blood. "You can't guarantee me anything; I'm not staying here."

When I turned and took a few steps into the forest, the king jogged up to me, sliding between me and my nonexistent destination. "Wait."

"No." I stopped anyway, because he was in my way.

"You need food, right? Clothing? Shelter? I can put you in my castle, make sure you're taken care of at least. I've been searching for you, you know. Ever since you disappeared."

"Sure you have," I drawled, stepping around him.

He slipped back in front of me, his hands out in front of him. "Really, I have. I've had people out looking for you since that day. I fell unconscious after I gave you my magic, and by the time I woke up, you'd already been taken."

I scowled. "Why would I believe you?"

"Because you tried to kill me, and I didn't stop you."

My hands found my hips, and I glowered at him. "You sensed my magic as I transformed and knew I wouldn't be able to kill you."

His lips twitched.

Was he fighting a grin?

Bastard.

"I did. But I still let you try."

"Get out of my way." I brushed past him, headed further into the forest.

He caught up to me, and walked at my side. "If you won't come into my castle, at least stay in this forest, where I know you're safe from my brother. Laith wouldn't take so kindly to the woman with his magic trying to end his life. And if he finds you, he'll use you against me."

I stopped. "Which one is he? Laith?"

It took the king a moment to realize what I was asking before he explained. "My brother; the Dark King."

Stars.

That was the one Vena was going after, and she was the gentlest of us.

My mind turned quickly, and I didn't speak for a few minutes.

"I can have food brought out to you, if you stay in the forest." The king took my silence for agreement, I supposed. "And bedding—I'm sure we can get something set up. A safe, comfortable place for you to stay. You wouldn't have to worry about hurting anyone, or anyone hurting you. It gets cold, but—"

"I'm used to the cold," I interrupted.

The king's expression darkened. "Where have you been? What's happened to you since I gave you my magic?"

Ignoring those last two questions, I stopped walking.

I needed information about the other kings, so I could rescue my friends from them if I needed to. They didn't know they wouldn't be able to kill the kings whose magic they held. And the best place for information? Their brother himself.

"Fine, I'll stay in your forest for now. I won't need your food, bedding, or shelter though."

"Okay." The king didn't call me on the lack of answer I gave him. But he also didn't leave.

"So, you can go." I gestured back toward his castle.

"Alright, then." The king turned around and strode back in the direction he'd come from. "My shadows dance here at night. Don't be scared," he called as he walked away.

"They're my shadows too," I called back, scowling in his direction.

As soon as he was gone, my scowl faded.

I stared into the large, empty forest, and my stomach clenched.

I didn't know how to hunt for food, or set up a shelter for myself. The only things I really knew how to do was survive torture, and talk my friends through their pain.

"What would the first step be?" I murmured to myself. A breeze blew through the trees, and my hands grew chilly as it cooled the blood on them. "Washing up, I suppose."

I had seen a stream near the place I'd entered the forest.

Turning, I headed back in that direction.

My arms wrapped around my abdomen as I walked, and I tried not to remember the fear on the faces of the fae the monster within me had attacked. The king had been right about me not wanting to hurt anyone, or to be hurt by anyone.

And he'd probably been right about me needing all of the things he offered, too.

I'd survive the forest though. I'd lived through far too much hell to lose my life to the damned woods.

It took a while, but I eventually found the stream. Stripping my shift dress off was quick, and left me in the simple,

strapless black undergarment that covered me from breast to
ass. It was one piece, the bottom coming to a close around
the tops of both of my thighs to keep me covered. I was
skinny after years of little food, but given the magic that ran
through my veins—the king's magic—I'd recover from the
years of suffering quickly.

Physically, at least.

Mentally... well, I wasn't sure there was anything to recover.

I leaned over the edge of the stream, scooping enough water
in my hand to wash the blood off my arms, face, and neck.
The water was ice cold, but as I'd told the king, I was used to
the cold.

That didn't mean I wanted to roll around in it, but I'd
survive.

It took some time to get the blood off my skin and out of my
hair, but I managed.

CHAPTER 4

WHEN I WAS CLEAN, I braided my hair messily. The chains I'd worn had never let me reach back far enough to do my hair, but Akari had taught me to braid before we went our separate ways.

Not seeing a reason to put my slip dress back on (I couldn't have cared less about modesty after the life I'd lived), I cleaned the bloody spots in the river and then carried it by a strap so I wouldn't get it dirty.

After finding a somewhat large clearing, with a view of the city's walls and the castle protruding above it, I hung my dress on a branch and sat down on a large rock, trying not to shiver as the cold seeped into my legs through the rock and the icy breeze that blew through the trees.

Staring out at the castle, I almost regretted turning the king's offer down.

Although, he wanted to use me to kill his brothers. And that made me regret it a lot less.

A few branches cracked a small distance in front of me, and some bushes parted enough to let a tall, strong man followed by his monstrous friend into the clearing.

The king, and Jesh.

They were both carrying massive bags on their backs, and had gigantic packs of what looked like some kind of poles and stakes in their hands.

And I was definitely still only wearing my underclothes. Which would've bothered me, had I not been chained in a small room wearing nearly nothing for so much of my life.

"What are you doing?" I asked the king, standing up. I itched to grab the golden dagger, but I'd lost it in the throne room.

"Setting up a tent." He flashed me a grin. "You didn't think I was going to listen to you, did you?"

Gratitude and annoyance both warred within me.

"Get used to it. The bastard doesn't listen to anyone," Jesh grumbled, setting his pack of poles down. "You tell him not to do something stupid, and what does he do? Something stupid."

"Like insisting on setting up a tent for a woman who tells him she's not interested?" I drawled.

Jesh gestured toward me. "Exactly. Exactly like this."

"I take care of my own. That's responsibility, not stupidity," the king drawled back, setting his own things down next to the ones Jesh had already dropped. He looked at me, then focused on Jesh. "I'll be back with the food and bedding. Keep an eye on my salvation, would you?" He flashed a grin my way before striding back into the forest.

"Was he talking about me?"

"Mmhm. You did save his life, though you were too young to realize you were doing it." Jesh grabbed the first bundle of poles, and began unwrapping them, spreading them out.

"I told him I wanted to be alone."

"As I said, being a king doesn't exactly lead one to learn how to listen. Add that to the debt he feels that he owes you, I don't think you'll be rid of Namir any time soon."

"Namir?"

"The king's name." Jesh nodded in the direction he had headed.

"Is he always so..." I trailed off, not having a word for what I was trying to say.

"Positive? Insistent? Stubborn? Yes to all three."

Damn.

I watched Jesh start to set up the tent, my eyes following the massive man. I'd never been attracted to anyone before—my captors and torturers had been far from desirable to me. But

I found my gaze following the movements of the man's arms, watching the way he worked.

"I don't think I got your name," Jesh remarked, as he continued.

"I don't think you did," I agreed.

He flashed me a smirk, but didn't argue.

"Is the woman you were with the king's lover?" I asked, after a few minutes of silence.

"If you don't want to share your name, why should I share intimate details about my king's court?" the man countered.

I bit back a sigh. "Diora. My name's Diora."

"Lav and Namir grew up together, and are practically siblings. Neither has any desire for one another that they've shared. Besides, the king waits for a fated bond."

My eyebrows lifted. "I thought those weren't common."

"They aren't."

Damn.

Well, I supposed that was a good thing. I wouldn't have to worry about him being attracted to me or anything.

"Why did you wait until now to seek him out?" Jesh asked, continuing to set up the tent. There were poles in the ground, pinning some kind of thick-looking fabric to the forest floor.

"This was the first opportunity I had," I admitted.

He continued setting up in silence, and I got the feeling he was waiting for me to explain more, to give him more information.

Despite my personal defenses, I'd never been asked about my past before. I'd never known friendship, outside of the friends I'd been chained in a room with.

"After the kings transferred their power into me and my friends, we were stolen by those who sought to take that magic from us. They didn't succeed—but not for lack of trying."

Jesh continued working in silence, not remarking on the words. I got the feeling that he didn't know what to say to that. Though my stomach curled a bit without knowing what he was thinking, I remained quiet.

He finished setting up the tent, which ended up being a white and silver structure that was larger than the prison cell my friends and I had spent my life in. The trees brushed the three corners at the top of the canvas, and I studied them silently.

Out in front of me, the bushes rustled again, and the king came walking into the clearing, his back and arms loaded up with more large bags and items.

He nodded toward me, striding past me and into the tent. Jesh was still adjusting some parts of the structure, but

Namir opened his bags and started setting things up.

I watched in confusion and fascination as he pulled out item after item. One of the largest was some type of thick roll, and another looked like a thick blanket. Though I didn't have names for all of the items, gratitude rolled through me with each new one I saw.

Jesh got to work setting up a second, smaller tent, off to the side of the large one. I didn't know why I'd need a second tent, but didn't want to end up in a conversation with the king I'd probably still need to find a way to kill.

The way Jesh moved had caught my attention, but Namir's fluid motions held me enthralled. I'd never imagined I could enjoy watching someone set up a tent or put things away, but damn.

Namir finished setting his items up and moved to help Jesh with the rest of his tent. I heard them speaking in low tones, quiet enough that I couldn't make out what they were saying.

When Jesh eventually left me with Namir, I noticed that the king's expression had grown dark and furious. His movements became sharp and jerky, his shadowy magic seeming to leak from his skin the way mine did before the monster in me took over.

Could he shift into a shadow wolf too?

Why was he furious?

I braced myself for torture, or a lecture, hating that it was my default expectation but unaware of a way to change that.

Eventually, he finished setting the second tent up and left, warning me to let him know if I needed anything else.

I waited until he was gone to get up off my rock and see what he and the other man had done.

Up on my feet, I wandered through the tents. The large one held a thick cushion, raised off the ground, with a couple of heavy, soft blankets resting on it. My fingers brushed them, and I marveled at the luxury.

The large tent also held a big box of food—dried fruit, vegetables, and meat, as well as a few different types of cheeses.

Pulling out a few small items, I held them in my hand as I continued to poke around at everything.

A silk bag in another corner held a handful of white and silver slip dresses similar to my black one but with softer fabric and more fancy details, as well as a few undergarments that were likewise comfier and more elegant than mine. I left them where they were, closing the drawstring on the bag so it'd stay sealed.

My fingers dragged over the thick white canvas of the tent as I made my way around it. There were decorative pillows all over the place, and I didn't know what they were there for, but they were soft and comfortable.

Slipping out of the large tent, I made my way to the second one. It was much, much smaller than the first. All there was room for within it was another one of the thick pads that I assumed were meant to be used as beds. It was lifted slightly off the ground, and there was a pile of heavy blankets as well as a pair of pillows on top of it. The blankets weren't at the same level of luxury as the ones in the large tent, and that made me feel slightly less out-of-place.

So, when I grew tired, I ate a few more of the dried food items before I zipped myself into the small canvas tent. Knowing I wouldn't be able to sleep in the undergarment I wore, I stripped that off and tossed it to the side of the strange bed before slipping under the blankets.

The soft fabric stroked my skin as I slid inside, the blankets soft and smooth in a way that nearly made me groan.

Was that comfort?

None of the inns had soft blankets like that, or thick cushions to lay on—was this a royalty thing?

Or was it just something everyone had, outside of inns?

I knew most fae had their own homes or apartments; did they all own blankets and cushions so comfortable?

It took a few moments for me to adjust to the newfound softness, but eventually I relaxed into the bedding and managed to fall asleep.

CHAPTER 5

My growling stomach woke me in the morning, and I stumbled out of the tent blearily. My gaze somehow managed to skip completely over the swaying smile-shaped fabric bundle tied between two trees as I beelined it toward the place I knew the food was located.

Plopping down on my ass on the floor, I tugged the lid off and pulled out some cheese and bread. After a few bites of each, I eyed the foods separately, and then stuck the cheese between two broken pieces of bread and bit down.

Yummm.

Footsteps sounded outside the tent, and I sighed inwardly.

The king ducked his head inside, and I froze.

His gaze landed on my face, sliding down my body a bit before he quickly lifted his eyes back to mine.

Stars.

I hadn't put clothes on.

My cheeks flushed; clothes were definitely required now that I was outside the prison.

"Naked early-morning snacking. Nice," Namir remarked.

If I wasn't so embarrassed, I would've been fighting a grin at the joke.

I glared instead, hoping it would get rid of him. "What are you doing here?"

"Invading a naked breakfast, it seems." He turned to face the forest, so he clearly wasn't checking me out. "Don't stop for my sake."

I cursed inwardly.

Why wasn't he leaving?

After swallowing my bite, I spoke again. "What are you doing out here, I meant? You own a castle, if I remember correctly."

"I told you, I protect what's mine."

My eyes drifted down his gorgeous, bare back, to the white pants he wore that clung to his backside.

I forced them upward, like he had.

"I am *definitely* not yours."

"The magic within you disagrees."

"Consider it mine, then. You can't kill your brothers, and I won't. So there's no way for me to be free of it, therefore it belongs to me."

"Why won't you kill them?" he countered.

Because they weren't mine to kill, honestly. They were Akari and Vena's.

I couldn't say that, though.

So instead, I drawled, "Life is sacred, remember? Death lands you on the sunny island that'll slowly drain you of life by disconnecting you from your magic permanently."

The king made a noncommittal noise. "I haven't ever sent anyone there. Seems unnecessarily cruel."

My eyebrows lifted. "Then what do you do with someone who ends the life of another?"

"Congratulate them or kill them myself, usually. In my experience, the only motivators for that kind of violence are self-defense or emotionless cruelty. In the case of self-defense, I make sure the killer has a safe home to live in, and that all other threats toward them have been destroyed. In the case of emotionless cruelty, I give the bastard a quick, painless death to protect the rest of my people."

"And what if you can't tell which it is?" I countered.

"Then my people dig until we've figured it out."

That didn't sound unreasonable to me. Not in the slightest.

"The scars on your wrists," the king said.

I didn't look at them, and didn't say anything about them either.

"Jesh told me what you said to him. That you were stolen by those who wanted to take my magic."

Of course he had.

Damn me for trusting him.

"He won't tell anyone else, but he and Lavee are the closest thing I have to family at this point. We don't keep secrets from each other." He paused. "Or at least, they don't keep secrets from me. My situation is... unique."

Still, I didn't say anything.

Jesh had broken my trust; he wouldn't get a second chance.

There were a few silent moments, and I finished my bread and cheese before easing myself to my feet. There was fancy clothing in the bag off in front of me, but I had no desire to flaunt the king's magic, or his attention.

Plus, white clothing made me slightly uncomfortable. The only time I'd seen anyone wear white in the first two decades of my life was when I was being tortured—and then, their clothes were always spotted with my blood. I'd been forced to get used to seeing people in white quickly after leaving the prison, but that didn't mean I wanted to wear the color.

"You're skin and bones. I saw the outline of your ribs—I've never seen that before."

"Glad to know you're comparing me to all of the other women you've bedded," I drawled, slipping past him and heading toward the small tent.

He chuckled, following me but remaining outside when I zipped myself into the small, comfortable space. It was warmer than the outside air, too, which was nice.

"I haven't bedded a woman before, Diora. As anyone in my portion of the court could tell you, I've been waiting for fate to speak to me."

"I don't know what that means."

It was a half-truth. I suspected I knew what it meant, but wasn't about to say it out loud.

"All fae have fated mates, most just aren't willing to find them, or wait for them. They pair up with someone they feel no soul-connection with, to avoid the possibility of being hurt. Unlike them, I seek the female that fate designates as mine."

"And how does a person know when they've found the one fate designates for them?" I slid into my undergarment while I spoke.

"They just know."

My eyes rolled. "Because that isn't vague."

He chuckled. "The connection is soul-deep, Diora. Does your soul come out and speak to you? Mine certainly doesn't."

"So you've saved yourself for her, mind, body, and soul."

"Yes."

I shook my head up at the ceiling, not believing that I was talking about fated mates with the man I was supposed to murder. "You can't expect her to have done the same for you."

"I don't," he agreed.

Though I waited for more of an explanation, it didn't come.

"Then why save yourself?" I finally asked, unzipping the tent and sliding my legs out first. My bare feet met the cold, rocky ground, and I tried not to shiver.

"Because when I meet her, I don't want her to question my dedication," he said simply. "I don't want her to wonder how she compares to previous partners, or to worry that she isn't enough."

"But you don't know if she *will* be enough."

His lips curved upward. "Love is a choice, Diora. I *choose* whether or not she's enough—and she will always be enough for me."

"I suppose she'll be a lucky woman then, won't she?" I crossed the clearing, snagging my dress off the branch and then tugging its opening over my head. It was dry, but cold.

"The big tent was meant to be yours." Namir gestured toward it. "I was going to sleep in the small one."

I shrugged. "You're the king; you take it." I headed back toward the food.

"There's warm breakfast in the castle. Oatmeal, and fresh fruit. Hot rolls, with jam," he remarked, following me into the large tent.

"Go ahead and eat, then." I sat down beside my dried food box.

He rolled his eyes at me. "I recall explaining that I'm not leaving."

"Send one of your other guards. Jesh has already proven himself skilled at extricating information from me; might as well give him another shot at learning whatever it is you want to know."

Namir sat down on the other side of the food box, and I tucked my legs up beside me, so his thighs wouldn't brush my feet. "He wasn't trying to extricate information."

I scowled at the king. "I thought he was trying to be my friend. Won't make that mistake again."

"He *was* trying to be your friend." Namir grabbed a bag of some type of dried fruit I didn't have a name for. I hadn't known what it was, so I hadn't tried it.

"You haven't touched the elmbins," he remarked, pulling a dried slice from the bag.

"I've never seen those before." I shrugged, still snacking on the dried bloodberries.

"Here." He broke off a piece on the end of the long slice, tossing it in his mouth before handing it to me.

The bastard knew exactly what he was doing; showing me it was safe to eat by having some himself before handing it over.

I reluctantly took it from him. "Is it sour?"

"A bit. Do you like sour food?"

"No. I'm not used to eating anything with much flavor. Just gruel, and more recently, stew."

His expression darkened. "Where did they keep you?"

I ignored the question, as I had the previous ones about my past. Not only did I not trust the king, but I didn't know for sure that he wouldn't hand me back to those of my captors who remained if he found out where I'd been.

There was no proof that he hadn't been working with them, after all.

Breaking off a piece of the dried fruit, I placed it on my tongue. The sour and sweet flavor had me cringing, and I handed the rest of the fruit back to the king.

"Not a fan?"

"No."

I grabbed a bottle of water from inside the box, unscrewing the lid and lifting it to my lips. The water washed the flavor from my tongue, and I recapped the bottle before setting it back down in the box.

"I'm training Jesh and Lavee to use their magic. I can teach you, too," he offered, breaking off another piece of his sour fruit while I returned to the bland bloodberries.

"No." There wasn't a chance in hell that I was going to test my magic in any way. When that happened, I lost control entirely, and ended up killing people.

"It can be controlled," Namir remarked. "I used to have the same problem."

"You transformed into a shadow wolf that ripped the throats out of anyone who came close?" I countered.

"No, I never transformed. But—"

"Then you know nothing of my problem." I stood, abandoning the berries. I was still hungry, but satiated enough that I'd prefer the silent peace of my tent to the king's stubborn positivity.

My gaze caught on the wide bit of fabric hanging from two trees, and I realized it had to be some kind of bed, and that Namir had to have slept in it.

Not allowing myself to consider his reasoning for doing so, I slipped back into the small tent and zipped it closed.

Namir didn't argue with my escape, or call me out for leaving. And soon enough, I heard talking out beyond my small sanctuary. It only took me a moment to put the voices to the faces, and confirm that they were Jesh and Lavee.

"Where's your violent ward?" Lavee asked. Though I scowled up at the top of the tent with her words, there didn't seem to be any ill-intent behind them.

I knew enough of society to know that a ward was someone a fae adopted and cared for, whether old or young, and I was *not* the king's ward.

"Diora is resting," the king said, generically. He could've come out and said I was avoiding him, for all I cared.

"Did you offer to teach her to use your magic?" Lavee checked. "Someone's got to, before she accidentally transforms into that shadow wolf and kills someone."

"She'll learn when she's ready," Namir said firmly.

Lavee scoffed. "Bullshit. She's a danger to all of us until she's learned control."

Jesh growled, "Lav, don't—"

My tent was yanked open, and the magic in my chest exploded into action.

Shadows burst from my skin as I transformed, and the monster didn't hesitate before it lunged for Lavee's throat.

She swore as her back crashed to the ground, and my wolf's teeth tore into her neck. Lavee's magic darkened the air around her, but my monster's shadows cut through it like it was nothing more than air.

Before the wolf could rip the other woman's throat out completely, a shadowed figure appeared between my monster and Lavee. His throat took the bite of her teeth without so much as flinching, since she didn't leave a damned mark, and he rolled her off of Lavee hard.

Namir's body became shadow as he and my wolf rolled, neither of their backs actually touching the rocks on the ground beneath them.

When they'd finally stopped rolling, my wolf was on top of Namir. His hands were tangled in her fur, holding on to the back of her head, his eyes burning into hers.

Blood dripped from her muzzle to his cheek, but he didn't flinch even as she snarled at him.

"Find your peace," Namir instructed the wolf.

Or was he talking to me?

She snarled again, and if I were in her place, I would've snarled too.

What peace? My life had been hell, and the only short relief I'd had from it had been those days my friends and I were in that inn.

We should've forgotten our revenge and freedom and run away to another land together instead, but it was too late.

I could only hope the other kings would be as understanding as Namir when my friends tried to kill them.

Shadows wrapped around us, circling Namir and my wolf, closing them into a bubble together. Though my wolf continued snarling at him, she didn't fight to get free of his grip on her fur, or his shadows.

They felt... comfortable, in a way I didn't have words to describe.

"Listen to the shadows," Namir instructed, his gray eyes still burning my wolf to the soul. "Hear them move, and whisper. Let them calm you."

My wolf's next snarl was half-hearted, and her eyes followed the movements of the shadows as they spun and twisted slowly above Namir's face.

Her head began to sway side to side, then up and down, and the magic that had been tensed in my chest began to relax slowly.

Finally, the protective shield over my heart shattered, and the wolf's form broke apart. I landed hard on Namir's chest, panting and swearing. His hands were wrapped around the back of my head, and he pulled my forehead lightly against his. The shadows still swirled around us, holding us in a soft, quiet bubble.

"That was good, Diora," he murmured. His lips were only a breath from mine, and my face twisted in another snarl.

"I probably *killed* your friend."

"Lavee is tougher than she looks. And she knew better than to scare a sleeping wolf, anyway." His voice was light, and soft, despite what had just happened.

I rolled off his chest, ignoring the pain in my head and body as I slammed to the ground. When I shoved at his shadows, they parted for me, and I stalked back to my small tent.

If it hadn't been nailed into the ground with the thick poles and stakes, I would've moved it.

Lavee was bloody and a bit pale when I passed her, but she was breathing, and her throat looked almost healed.

Jesh nodded at me, and I scowled at him too.

That bastard was *not* my friend; none of them were.

I needed to figure out a way to kill Namir and get out of there, before my monster took over again and then ravaged the entire damn city. Namir might be able to stop her for a while, but he hadn't seen the full extent of her magic.

The damage she could do...

Stars, it was terrifying.

Even if I couldn't kill the king, I needed to get far from the city.

So I zipped myself into the tent and carefully stripped out of my even-more-ripped dress, using the dirty, bloody silk to wipe my face before tucking it underneath the comfortable mattress I'd claimed for the time being.

Eventually, he would fall asleep or go back to the castle. And then I would slip away, so I couldn't hurt anyone else.

CHAPTER 6

THEY WALKED FURTHER AWAY before resuming their practice. No one mentioned my transformation or my wolf's attack; at least, not when they were close enough for me to hear them speaking.

After they moved, their voices were caught in the wind, barely a murmur when they reached me.

I remained in my tent, staring up at the top of the thing and trying to sleep for the rest of the afternoon. I never managed to fall asleep though, and eventually, my hunger dragged me back outside.

I ate more bread, cheese, and dried fruits and vegetables, avoiding the sour one Namir had been eating and a few others with strong flavors. The voices of Namir and his friends, along with the sounds of their swords clanging, were a bit clearer without the canvas blocking them out. I tried not to listen, but couldn't help that I heard a few of their words.

"Good, Jesh," Namir approved. "Remember, it should be an extension of your own body. See it like a hand, and it'll move like a hand."

"It's not a damn hand," Jesh growled back.

My lips quirked upward, just a tiny bit.

Maybe Namir's was, but my magic certainly wasn't a damn hand.

"The way you see it determines how it makes itself known," Namir countered. "When it comes to magic, almost everything is in your head."

"I can't make myself turn into a damned wolf," Lavee shot back.

Namir chuckled. "No, you don't possess enough for that. But you can still do a hell of a lot with what you've got."

Their swords clashed, and their instructions and arguing continued.

Namir's words stuck with me, though.

See it like a hand, and it'll move like a hand.

I held my own hand out, and imagined the shadows that leaked from my skin before my wolf took over engulfing it, forming a hand of their own.

Slowly, my shadowy magic slid out of my pores, wrapping around my fingers.

My lips parted when the shadows conformed perfectly to every line of my palm, wrist, and arm, forming a dark gray, misty glove.

Shock tore through me, and the shadows became a knife in my palm. When that shock turned to terror, the power clenched in my chest.

The monster wanted to break out, to break free.

I grabbed my water bottle out of the box and lifted it to my lips, chugging the liquid down in hopes that it'd drown my panic.

It didn't remove the feeling altogether, but my stress and fear did fade as I drank. Slowly, my shoulders and body began to relax.

I definitely needed to get away from the city, though.

Far, far away.

Making up my mind to leave later that night, after Namir went back to his castle or back to sleep, I grabbed one last handful of dried food before crossing the now-small clearing and slipping back into the tent I'd claimed.

My black dress was ripped and bloody in too many places to bother bringing it along, but if I was living in the forest, I could do so without an overdress. I would find edible plants to keep me alive, hopefully. Hunting animals was something fae only did in the absolute worst of times, and I had no desire to do that. So, edible plants would have to do.

Maybe I could make my way back toward the inn my friends and I were going to meet at. I couldn't stay there—didn't have the funds, or the self-control—but being nearby would mean I could find my friends sooner, if they got there earlier than the year we'd planned.

Deciding that was as good a plan as any, I remained in my tent for the rest of the afternoon and evening, snacking slowly on what little food I'd brought back with me.

I heard Namir moving around after he finished training with Jesh and Lavee, and I finally managed to doze off while he was rustling through the food box, eating.

THE NEXT TIME I woke up, I felt like a few hours had passed. It was the middle of the night, but I'd slept enough through the day that my internal clock was a bit off.

Listening closely, I tried to see if I could hear Namir moving around.

Nothing.

A few more minutes passed while I waited, just to make sure.

I didn't hear a damn sound.

Right.

That was as good a time to go as any.

I slipped out of my tent, planning to claim I was just headed out to pee in the trees if Namir was still out there after all.

But sure enough, when I stepped out, he wasn't anywhere to be seen.

The large fabric stretched between the trees was swinging, though. And when I looked closer, I thought I could see the basic outline of a guy inside it.

Taking care to move silently, I slipped out into the forest behind the tent.

My magic swelled a bit as I stepped further into the darkness of the forest. I put my hand on the center of my chest, trying to calm the beast within me as I pressed forward.

The further I went, the darker the forest became—and the more shadows I began to notice. They were wrapped around the trees, draped through the leaves. Dancing in the wind, entwined in the flowers, and embedded in the dirt.

My footsteps slowed the further I walked, but not because my fear grew. Actually, the more I walked, the calmer I became.

The shadows started to tease me, brushing up against me every now and then, whispering soft, comforting words to me.

Eventually, I slowed to a complete stop. The shadows danced around me, tickling my skin and playing with my hair. My eyes closed, my lips tilting upward as I let them slip over me, embracing me like a long-lost friend.

I wasn't good at physical contact—the only contact I'd ever known until a few days earlier was at the hands of my torturers. To say I didn't like to be touched was an understatement.

But the shadows' embrace wasn't a touch; it was a hug, a blanket over my underprepared and overstimulated mind and body.

Footsteps sounded behind me, and I felt the shadows change slightly. They murmured to me in words I couldn't translate, but somehow, the feeling came through.

Namir was behind me, they were saying.

They released me slightly, and I let my feet turn as they slowly spun me around to face him.

The king approached, his expression one of unmistakable interest.

"I'm leaving," I told him.

The shadows whispered to me, and the desire to stay swelled in my chest. They wanted me to stay—they thought I *needed* to.

"That's fine." Namir didn't look fazed by my statement at all.

That made things easier, I guessed. Though the shadows were comfortable, and calming, they weren't alive. And if they were, I probably shouldn't trust them. So I was sticking with my plan, which meant leaving.

I nodded at Namir, and turned back toward the forest.

The shadows remained wrapped around my arms and waist, dancing lightly through my hair and over my chest.

Rather than letting me leave him, Namir fell into step beside me.

I tried not to glare at him, and hoped that if I was quiet for long enough, he'd just leave.

Time passed, and we both continued walking.

He didn't leave.

"What are you doing?" I finally asked him.

"Going with you." He flashed me a small grin, but I didn't turn to look at him, so our eyes didn't meet. "Even if I wanted to let you walk away, the shadows are urging me to stay close."

"So you're not making them do this?" I checked, gesturing to my arm, which was wrapped in shadows.

He chuckled. "No. It'd feel different if I was doing it; more like a physical touch. I've never seen them react like this to anyone, though. Myself included."

That was... odd.

"Why?"

"I'm not sure," he admitted, his gaze curious as he walked beside me, his eyes following me. "If I had to guess, I'd say it's probably because my personal magic was always more intimately connected to the shadows than the court's magic, which I currently possess. So the shadows probably feel like you're one of them. Their queen, even."

I didn't hate the idea of being a shadow. Staying under everyone's radar, completely untouchable. No one could hurt me if I didn't want to be hurt, or find me if I didn't want to be found.

The freedom... stars, I would give anything for that kind of freedom.

"Make your shadows touch my arm then, so I know the difference," I countered, deciding to ignore that last fact about being the shadows' queen.

He glanced over at me, and a ribbon of shadow stretched off Namir's arm, reaching for my bare palm. The ribbon shifted in the air, becoming a shadowed version of Namir's hand.

His shadowed fingers slipped between mine, and a shiver ran down my spine. It felt... warm. Soft. Blissful.

"Damn," I remarked, withdrawing my hand from the shadowed one.

Namir pulled it away, flashing me a knowing smile. "You asked."

"How did you know it would feel different, though?" I countered. "You said the shadows don't interact with anyone else like this."

He didn't answer immediately.

I narrowed my eyes at him.

"You probably don't want to know this answer," he told me. "But to be honest, your shadows feel different to me than these ones." He gestured to the ones playing with my hair and dancing around me. "They feel warm, and comfortable."

Double damn.

"Thank you for being honest," I said, turning my face back to the forest. Though I wasn't sure what to think about his words, I knew that I never wanted to be lied to again. I'd had more than enough lies to last me a lifetime while I was chained. My abusers had teased and taunted me, given hope and then taken it away as another form of their torture.

"Of course." Namir sounded surprised, but didn't ask for details about why I was so grateful for his honesty.

"You can still leave, you know," I told him, wanting to make sure he knew as well as I did that he was free to leave. He seemed to think he needed to follow me, or something. "If I die, it won't be on your conscience. I chose to leave, and you don't owe me anything. Your magic saved my life, even if it destroyed it too."

"I know." He left it at that, his voice almost amused.

"You know what?"

"That I can leave. I'm following you by choice, remember?"

Right.

"But why?" I pressed. "I just freed you of all responsibility."

He chuckled. "You can't free me of my conscience, Diora. I'm here because I want to be, and I'm trying to teach you magic because I want to see you learn. I don't want you to fear the shadows; they've become a part of you."

"A part of me I'd like to be free of," I grumbled.

He chuckled. "I think we all have those parts of us."

I scowled. "I can't imagine the Shadow King has any part of himself he'd like to be free of. Look at you." I gestured to his abdomen, and he glanced down.

"I'm not sure what you see, but I'm just a man. I've struggled with my magic, same as anyone, but on a much larger scale. I carry a hatred for one of my brothers that I wish I could be free of. My determination to wait for my true mate has earned me much scorn and disapproval from those who both support me and despise me. And there are still nights where I don't sleep, because when I close my eyes, my mother's hatred stares back at me," he said honestly.

The amount of truthful, vulnerable information he had just handed me made me stop in my tracks.

I turned, and looked at him.

Just... looked.

He looked back.

After a few moments of silence, his lips curved upward. "Looks like I've stunned you to silence with my honesty this time."

I tried to scowl, but couldn't.

So instead, I turned and continued my walk into the forest.

He kept walking beside me.

I wasn't going to hand him all of my truths like he had handed me his—I definitely wasn't there yet.

But I could give him one thing.

"I don't dream," I said, my gaze focused on the forest in front of me. "My entire life has been a nightmare. I suppose the kings of sleep pity me enough not to haunt me while I'm unconscious."

Namir's fists clenched at his sides, and shadows leaked from his skin. He didn't say anything, though—and I didn't push him to.

Instead, we just continued walking.

CHAPTER 7

Eventually, I grew too tired to keep going. Picking out a mossy spot that didn't look incredibly lumpy, I stepped off the path I'd been creating.

"You're going to sleep here?" Namir asked, lifting an eyebrow at me. "There's no bed."

"Then it'll be just like my childhood," I drawled, plopping down on my ass on the moss. "Cold, a little wet, and extremely uncomfortable."

Namir's expression darkened, and he sat beside me. "Moss it is."

"We're not sharing," I warned him.

"What is there to share?" he asked, gesturing to the moss. "No bed, remember?"

"Go home, Namir," I said with a sigh. "You're clearly not made for the discomfort of the forest."

He scowled at me. "You're not *made* for discomfort either, Diora."

Deciding not to argue, I draped myself over the moss, leaving him enough space to lay on it too. "Don't touch me. I don't like to be touched."

"Alright." He didn't sound upset about the revelation, and I didn't get the impression that he was going to get handsy or anything.

As I closed my eyes and tried to relax, the cold of the moss seeped into my skin.

Trying hard not to shiver, I ignored both the chilly moss, and the icy wind that slowly blew through the trees. Bumps broke out on my skin, as they always did when I got cold, but I ignored that as always.

The shadows continued to swirl around me, comforting me, but they weren't warm. Not in the slightest.

I tried to rest anyway.

"I can't sleep with your teeth chattering," Namir grumbled at me. "Either let me hold you, or let me wrap my shadows around you."

I scowled into the forest. "No thanks."

He grunted at me. "You're so damn stubborn."

"Says the bastard who followed me into the forest after I told him to turn around multiple times," I spat back. "Just go to sleep."

My eyes closed in frustration, and I fought like hell to stop myself from shivering.

A few minutes later, I heard his teeth start chattering too.

Dammit.

I had to pick one of the options; sleeping in his arms, or wrapped in his shadows.

Neither option sounded great, to be honest. Both would probably bring up feelings I didn't want to deal with—and both would feel much more intimate than I was comfortable with.

But even that intimacy was better than freezing to death.

His shadows had felt less intimate than I imagined an actual touch would, but if he wrapped me in his shadows, he would still be cold. And I'd feel like shit if I snored away, warm and wrapped in his magic, while he shivered beside me.

So I sighed. "Fine. We can lay together. It's only for body heat though—I don't want you confessing to your damn fated mate that I seduced you into snuggling with me or anything when you finally meet her."

"That's not going to be a problem."

I rolled to face him, my eyes narrowed at him. "You have no idea. I've heard that mates are extremely possessive."

"Shouldn't you be worried that *your* fated mate will hunt me down after you tell him about this?" he gestured between us.

I rolled my eyes. "I'll die long before I meet my fated mate."

He narrowed his eyes at me, then. "Don't talk like that."

"Why shouldn't I? Your magic already earned me twenty-one years of torture; it's a miracle I'm not dead already."

"It's not a *miracle*. You're not dead because you're fucking strong, Diora. Take the credit for your survival."

The emotion in his words surprised me.

"Fine, alright." I turned away from him, not wanting him to see the shock in my eyes. His chest pressed to my back, and my eyes widened when I felt something hard against the top of my ass.

Stars.

Was that his erection?

Akari was the only one of us old enough to know how all of the baby-making shit worked when we were taken, but she'd explained it all to me and Vena when I was a teenager. It wasn't like I'd seen the male anatomy though; it was all just theoretical to me.

At least, until his erection was jabbing my backside.

Not sure what I'd say about that, I decided just to keep my mouth shut. Namir didn't mention it either, so that made it easier.

His arm draped over my waist, and surprisingly, it wasn't uncomfortable. Honestly, it was far from uncomfortable.

It was... nice.

Really nice.

Not that I'd say so out loud.

I was too stunned to mention that, anyway, or to allow myself to overthink the situation.

My eyes closed, but I was still shivering a bit. He must've noticed, because a moment later, shadows began to slide off his skin, slowly engulfing us both.

I felt my own shadows respond, and kept my eyes closed.

We both relaxed further as the comfortable, peaceful warmth wrapped around us, and eventually, I fell asleep.

WHEN THE MORNING CAME AROUND, I woke up first. Namir's erection was still pressed against my backside, and I wanted to get up before we had an awkward conversation about that. So, I slipped out of his arms, pressing on his shadows to convince them to release me.

Though they seemed reluctant, they finally parted, and I slipped out of the blissfully-warm cocoon we'd created for ourselves.

The morning air was brisk, so I wrapped my arms around my abdomen as I peered up at the moon. It was a crescent, at the moment. And damn, I loved the way it reflected across the stars. It reminded me of Akari—she held the Night King's magic, and when she used her magic, she glowed like the moon's light.

The shadows came out to meet me again, though there were far fewer of them than there had been while we walked during the night. My lips curved upward, my eyes closing while they tugged at my hair and wrapped softly around my torso.

A groan came from the shadowed bubble behind me, and I didn't turn around as Namir stumbled to his feet.

"I hate mornings," he grumbled to me, shoving messy strands of dark hair out of his eyes. "Have I ever told you that?"

I bit back a snort. We'd only known each other a couple of days, and had only had real conversations two or three times. "No."

"I'm sure you'll hear it again. Jesh tells me the only things he expects from me are my stubbornness and my hatred for mornings."

"I agree with him on the stubbornness," I tossed back.

"Are we heading back to the castle?" Namir glanced around the forest, as if trying to regain his bearings.

No.

Maybe?

I hadn't decided.

"I'll tell you when I figure that out."

Namir nodded agreement, walking beside me without complaint. "Did you bring any of that dried fruit?"

I wished the answer was yes, but I'd been too determined to sneak out.

"I'll take that as a no." He bobbed his head. "I know what we can eat out here. We'll be fine."

At least there was that.

WE WALKED ALL DAY. When I asked if anyone would worry about him being gone, he brushed it off with an explanation that he always disappeared once a week or so, for peace and quiet. And that since the people who would worry about him knew we couldn't kill each other, they wouldn't wonder whether or not he was alive.

I figured that was as good an answer as any, so I kept walking. We weren't really headed anywhere specific, just weaving through the forest. And we didn't see any predators or large animals coming for us; I assumed they were scared off by the magic that emanated from both of us.

"So, the scars," Namir said, as the day began to end. It was almost time to stop for sleep, but I was putting it off, because sleep meant snuggling with the king again.

And despite his words, I did still think his fated mate would mind him cuddling with me.

My defenses rose. "What about them?"

"Where else are you scarred?" he checked.

I scowled. "Why?"

"Because clearly, you were chained. I'd like to know where."

My scowl turned into a scoff. "If I tell you, you won't prod for more answers?"

"I won't."

"Fine. My wrists, ankles, and waist." I dragged a finger over my abdomen, the location I had memorized by heart. Not because of the scar that circled me there, but because of the golden cuff that had wrapped around me for so much of my life.

"Stars, Diora," he growled at me a bit.

My defenses rose. "I didn't volunteer to be there."

"I'm not growling at you, I'm growling at them." He tossed a hand toward the forest, out in front of us. "Who are they? Where are they? Let me end their stars-fucking lives."

My defenses didn't vanish, though I did relax slightly. "Most of them are dead already."

He shot me a questioning look.

"When we escaped, we... I... they're mostly dead," I said hastily, wanting to talk my way out of the discussion as quickly as possible.

"I'm going to need more information than that," the king warned.

I flashed him a glare. "You're not getting it."

"Diora," he warned.

"Namir," I mimicked his tone.

He huffed. "You're so damned stubborn."

"I suppose we have that in common, then." My fists clenched at my sides, and I forced myself to keep breathing evenly, to prevent my monster from forcing her way out. She couldn't hurt Namir, but that didn't mean I wanted her to take control.

"At least tell me if it's anyone I know; anyone close to me," the king prodded.

"How would I know whether or not you've met them?" I tossed back. "I was chained, remember?"

"You can use the shadows to show me your memories of their magic, to give me an impression of who they are."

I scowled. "I'm not using the shadows for a damned thing, *King*. End of discussion."

Namir grumbled, but we kept walking.

THAT NIGHT WAS EVEN MORE awkward than the first. We didn't really talk, and both of us were stiff as we shared body heat without really cuddling. We got up before the morning came around, both of us restless and a bit grumpy.

As we continued to walk, I grew snappy, and he grew quiet. He didn't seem offended by my snappiness, though he probably should've been. And he never tried to force me to go back to the castle—though he probably should've.

We wandered the forest for nearly a week before I finally admitted to myself that I didn't like sleeping under the stars, or on moss. My feelings for the king I slept with were mixed, and guarded, but I didn't hate sleeping at his side as much as I hated the dampness of the moss beneath me or the uneven harness of the rocks around us.

The small tent that the king had set up for me was calling me.

And as he remarked on multiple occasions, I could always leave again if I wanted to. So, I finally told him I wanted to go back to the tents, and he led the way. They were close—less than two hours away—and I was suspicious that he might've been leading me in a circle somehow.

But, I was glad that we'd made it back to the tents, so I said nothing.

AFTER WASHING myself and my undergarments in the creek, I pulled the wet clothing back on long enough to walk back to the tents.

When I got there, I found the small tent's flaps hanging open —and I found Namir passed out in the bed.

Damn him.

With a sigh, I padded over to the large tent. Really, the whole thing was ridiculous.

But when I slipped out of my underclothing and tucked myself into the blankets, my eyes closed at the soft luxury of the fabric. I fought back a groan at the feel of it on my skin.

And it only took a few moments before I was snoring away, dead to the world.

CHAPTER 8

WHEN I WOKE UP, it took a few moments to reorient myself to the world around me. I was in the large tent, but it was darker than it had been when I fell asleep—I hadn't closed the flaps to the tent, but they were definitely closed now.

The room was cool, dark, and quiet.

To anyone who hadn't grown up as I had, it would've felt peaceful.

But my mind immediately flashed to my past

I scrambled out from beneath the blankets, crashing to the ground and then clawing my way back to my feet. My power flooded me, and I was engulfed by shadows in an instant. My monster charged at the side of the tent, tearing her way through the canvas walls. The light off the full moon illuminated the clearing, but the shadow wolf only saw one thing:

Threats.

A handful of them, gathered near the hanging fabric that the king had slept in until he took my tent.

They all spun to look at her, at my monster, and a few shocked murmurs ripped through the crowd.

She barreled toward them, barely noticing the dark-haired king and his two closest companions standing at the front of the group.

Lavee barked, "Give the king space," and Jesh enforced it with his gigantic form.

Namir lunged for my wolf as she threw herself at the crowd, her fangs bared and her shadows darkening, thickening.

She slammed into the king, and together they crashed to the rocky dirt. Never losing steam for a moment, the pair rolled, shadows fighting shadows.

My shadows were screaming, yelling, demanding blood, revenge, and death. His were whispering, but somehow, the whisper of his power seemed even louder than the scream of mine.

"Safety," the shadows whispered. "Security," they said. "Peace," they continued. "Mate," they added.

The words were on a constant, soft loop.

Safety.

Security.

Peace.

Mate.

Safety.

Security.

Peace.

Mate.

Safety.

Security.

Peace.

Mate.

Mate?

My roaring heart skipped a beat, or six.

The shadows engulfing me, giving life to the monster that lived within me, were sucked back into my body as if by some living force.

I rolled away from Namir, rocks and dirt cutting into my bare knees as I straightened and gasped for air, clutching at my chest, at my throat, at my head.

"What did you do?" I snarled at him, as he kneeled in front of me, holding his hands out with his palms toward me. His shadows had vanished too, his magic dissolved into the air.

"Nothing." There was honesty in his voice.

"You spoke through the shadows," I snarled. "I heard them speaking to me. Calling me mate."

Shocked murmurs tore through the crowd, and my attention jerked to them.

The magic within me swelled again, fiercer and angrier and so much more panicked.

"Diora." Namir's voice was firm but calm as he reached out and caught my wrist. Instinct told me to rip it from his grasp, but he placed it against the center of his chest, my palm to his bare skin, and then he let go.

The thrum of his heartbeat below my palm grounded me, somehow. I'd felt it night after night in the forest—it had calmed me then. Miraculously, it did the same still.

"Do you feel that?" His murmur was soft, but confident. Our eyes were locked; my golds, and his grays.

I jerked my head in a nod, hesitating for a moment before saying, "The shadows..."

"I wasn't speaking to them, or through them."

Stars.

We were *fated*?

"Leave us," Namir commanded, his eyes never leaving mine as his voice raised. Even without looking at them, I knew he spoke to the group gathered near the place he used to sleep, and not to me.

"You heard the king," Lavee growled. I knew she didn't like me—my monster had nearly killed her the week before. But she still followed Namir's order.

My golds remained locked with his grays as the crowd left, neither of us speaking again until the clearing was filled with only me, Namir, and our shadows. My heart pounded rapidly, sweat soaking my armpits and forehead as panic clutched my chest tighter and tighter. All I had on was my undergarment, still, and it was still damp from the wash the night before.

"Fated bonds are rare," I finally said, shaking my head harshly. "We can't be fated. I only just got free. I'm supposed to kill you—I have to, if I want true freedom. If I want to live."

My palm left his chest.

I stood swiftly, and then began to pace. Despite my stress, the monster in my chest remained mostly dormant, as if she had known and was confirming that Namir and I were connected.

80   LOLA GLASS

Namir changed the subject abruptly, standing too. His hands fell to his sides. "What happened in the tent, Love?"

I scowled at him and the damned nickname he'd just thrown at me, and continued pacing.

He stepped into my path, and his hand landed gently on the side of my arm. I halted, and his eyes crashed into mine again. "What happened in the tent, Diora? I haven't seen you that terrified since the first day we met."

A bead of sweat trailed down my back, making me shudder, and the king released my arm.

"Please," he told me. "I've been fighting the protective urges I feel for you since that first day we met, but your fear had me nearly turning into a shadowed wolf myself. What happened?"

I forced my eyes closed, and let out a slow breath.

Despite my confusion, and shock, and everything else, I trusted him.

Mostly.

So I explained, "Someone closed it—it was dark, and cold, and the same size as my prison." A shiver tore through my spine, and the beast in me stirred. "I thought I felt my chains, for a moment."

The king's expression darkened, as it always did when we spoke about my past. "You're safe with me, Diora."

"So your shadows have said." I pushed wild, tangled waves of hair off my face and out of my eyes.

At least my monster hadn't made anyone bleed this time.

"The small tent will be yours again, unless you wish to sleep together." His expression was still gravely serious, his body tenser than it should've been.

Shock hit me, then. "In the forest, when we slept on the moss. You knew we were fated."

The king's confident expression didn't waver. "I wouldn't have held you if you weren't mine. But you wouldn't have believed me if I told you—you had to determine our connection yourself."

I hated him for being right about that.

I hated the whole situation, actually.

The king had been waiting for his fated mate.

I had been searching for freedom, planning to kill once again for the sake of it.

Now the king had found me, but I refused to let go of the freedom I had fought so desperately to gain.

"This changes nothing for me," I warned.

His lips curved upward slightly. "I'd be surprised if it did."

Good.

At least he knew me well enough for that.

"We won't share a bed; I am not your possession. There may be a connection between us, but the bond won't develop without encouragement, and I won't encourage it. Fate can go to hell for all I care."

His lips curved upward further. "Whatever you say, Love."

My eyes narrowed at him, and his smile turned into a full-out grin.

"Why are you grinning at me?" I growled at him.

His grin widened. "I've been looking for you for more than twenty years, and waiting for you for nearly forty. You may not encourage the bond, but I sure as fuck will."

I blinked at him once, and then again.

A scowl twisted my features, and I stalked off toward the small tent.

His chuckle behind me warmed my chest more than I would ever admit, and my stomach clenched when he called after me, "Fight it as much as you want, Mate. I'll worm my way into your heart one way or another."

The small tent's flaps closed behind me, and I dropped into the bed. My damp clothing frustrated me so much that I ripped the undergarment off, accidentally tearing the fabric in the process. The torn clothing went under the mattress, where the torn dress probably still was.

I collapsed onto the pillow, hoping for peace. But the moment I tugged the blankets over my bare skin, Namir's scent hit me so hard that I nearly groaned.

How did he smell so damn good?

Stars, he was infuriating.

I forced my eyes to close, despite the pounding in my chest and the emotions racing in my mind. I couldn't sleep, but having my eyes closed helped calm me slightly.

There were too many things to think through, to process.

Namir had waited for his mate.

I was his mate.

Forcing my breaths to come out and in evenly, I reminded myself what I knew about fated pairs.

Akari hadn't said a whole lot—she said the couples were too rare for much of the information to be common knowledge.

But what she had said...

A fated pair was a couple that had been matched together by something bigger and more important than the gods of our world, Bluhm. There were many different lands and creatures on our planet, including gods who lived in a realm connected to it, and we all had some things in common.

But fated mates were bigger than our world, or our gods. Fated mates were determined by some deity in or beyond the stars, that nothing and no one could control or truly connect with. Some called that deity Fate, some called it God, some called it Destiny. Regardless of its name, it was the one thing in our world and all of the others that nothing and no one could change or alter.

Fate was the most common title given to it in our land and the Solar Provinces, according to Akari. She was a solar fae, so she had grown up there for most of her early life, and knew more about their land than the Dark Court we resided in.

What I knew about fated mates... no magic could alter their connection. The actual bond between them took time to develop, and as it developed, the mates grew more possessive and more protective. Akari had heard that their magic began to connect and combine as their bond grew, but she wasn't positive whether or not that was true. Same with the idea that their minds could connect and communicate as their bond strengthened; she had heard it, but the connection was so rare that there were very few people who knew whether or not it was true.

Had the power transfer situation somehow urged Fate to connect us? Or had we been connected even before Namir's magic became mine?

I had been so young then, that I supposed it didn't really matter if we had been connected before or after the power transfer. I'd been a dying, powerless infant—there would have been no life for me without Namir.

And that seemed significant to me, somehow.

My mind continued to spin, even as my stomach growled. After a few minutes, there was a knock against one of the thick poles that held the tent up.

I frowned at it.

Akari had spoken of people knocking on doors; was this the same?

"I can hear your stomach growling, Diora. You need to keep eating if you're going to continue gaining strength now that you're free," Namir warned.

"I'm hardly free," I retorted.

There was a long pause. "If you were to ask me, I'd say that having me at your side will make you more free. You wouldn't have survived in the forest so long without me pointing out which foods were safe to eat; you would've frozen nearly to your death if I wasn't there to hold you and warm you."

He went on, his voice growing lower as he spoke from the other side of the tent's flaps, "You fear being trapped again or hurt again, but you know that fated mates grow possessive and protective of each other. With the King of Shadows holding you close, keeping you safe, no one would touch you. If they so much as tried, I would destroy them—and take great pleasure in doing so." His voice was a growl, and barely above a whisper, with those last words and the ones that followed. "You fear losing control of your magic, but with me next to you, you never will because I'll be there, holding you, until you've regained that control."

My stomach clenched, and I said nothing.

The next time he spoke, his voice was raised again. "Take all the time you'd like to think about it, but if you don't eat, I will climb into that tent with you and force the food between your lips. And I can assure you, I will take great pleasure in doing so."

A scowl twisted my mouth. I shoved the tent's flap to the side and held a hand out. "Give me the food."

His lips curved up in a wicked yet somehow playful grin as he bent over, putting his face level to mine, and handed the plate over. "You're sexy when you're furious, Love."

I ripped the tent's flap back into place, glaring at the fabric and earning another chuckle from him.

Bastard.

The plate was loaded with hot food, though—more than I'd ever eaten at once, I was fairly certain.

My stomach growled in response, but I forced myself to pick up the fork resting on the plate.

Despite the beast in my chest, and the animalistic tendencies of the fae like me, I was civilized. I would eat with the damn fork.

Slowly and with much annoyance, I used the utensil to work my way through the food. The taste of it was like nothing I'd ever had before—the flavors intense. Nothing was too sour, or too sweet, and with every new type of food I tried, I became more convinced that this was a meal that might finally make me dream for the first time in my life.

And a dream about food was something worthwhile to hope for, I decided.

When I'd finished the food, I slipped the plate out of the tent and set it on the ground without opening the flaps or stepping out myself.

As I did, my hand brushed a warm stretch of skin, and I dropped the plate like it was a damned monster.

A warm hand caught mine gently as the plate crashed to the ground. Namir's shadows wrapped around my wrist immediately, calming me and making my eyes close.

"It's just me," he murmured.

Again with that.

"Just the Shadow King?" I drawled, wrestling my blissed-out eyes open.

He chuckled. "Yes."

I withdrew my hand. He released it, though I was fairly certain I sensed some reluctance as he did so. "What are you doing out there?"

"You may not have noticed, Love, but you're naked. And my court is full of very, very curious fae who keep attempting to sneak out here to see the fated mate their stubborn king has waited so long to meet. I'd hate to have to kill them for catching a glimpse of those perfect breasts."

My eyes widened, my face flushing. "You wouldn't."

"Oh, I would." His voice was playful, but there was a level of certainty behind the words that made me sure he was telling the truth.

I sputtered, "Why?"

"A man doesn't wait to meet his mate for as long as I have with the intention of sharing his female."

Stars.

"You're insane," I snapped, making sure the tent was closed tightly.

"Sanity is overrated," he said, his voice flooded with humor.

Shaking my head, I lowered myself to the mattress that smelled so deliciously like the man outside the tent. "I'm going to sleep. If you stick so much as a finger in this tent uninvited, you can consider our connection voided."

He chuckled. "I wouldn't dream of it."

As much as I wished I didn't, I believed him.

Despite everything, he had never lied to me or tried to force my hand.

And as much as I didn't want to, I trusted him.

Stars, I hated that.

And loved it, at the same time.

CHAPTER 9

NAMIR WOKE me up to eat a few hours later, with a ticklish touch of a shadowy tendril against my cheek. I hoped I'd fall back asleep after I ate, but when my stomach was full of the incredible hot food someone had brought us, I wasn't tired in the slightest.

"I'm coming out," I told Namir, knowing he was still sitting right outside. There was still a tendril of his shadows waving back and forth in the tent, brushing my skin every now and then.

"Put these on, then." I heard fabric rustling, and then his hand slipped through the tent's flaps, holding a thick silver bag.

I grimaced at it, but took it.

Opening the flap that hung over the top to close it, I peered into the bag.

White fabric with silver decorative embroidery.

My stomach clenched, and I closed the bag. I tossed it back through the tent's flaps, crashing back to the mattress. "Never mind."

There was a moment's pause. "Is something wrong with the clothes?" Namir's voice was surprised, and I heard him grab the bag, rustling around in it. "It just looks like a dress and undergarment. It feels comfortable; I told Lavee to get you whatever would feel the best against your skin."

My face twisted in a grimace, and I debated keeping my mouth shut.

"Diora?" He practically growled at me. "Tell me the problem."

I scowled at the top of the tent. "I don't want to look like the people who trapped me."

There was a long pause before he finally said, "I'll be back in a few minutes. Don't leave."

A moment later, I heard his quiet footsteps on the dirt, and closed my eyes. If I'd really wanted to, I could've made a run for it. I could get far enough into the forest to hide from him, and as long as I could get myself worked into a fearful frenzy, I could force my monster to take over and run us far, far away. After a week in the forest with Namir, I knew what plants were edible and which ones I shouldn't touch.

I could've run.

...But I didn't.

After a few minutes, his footsteps were on the dirt again. As he reached my tent, he asked, "Are you still there?"

I murmured my confirmation.

"Lavee will go out and find you some black clothing if you'd like, but we thought you might rather choose your own."

The words caught me off guard.

I hadn't expected that to be an option.

"What would you prefer, Love?"

I blinked once, and then again.

And then a third time.

My throat swelled.

He didn't push me for an answer, though, or demand I reply quickly. He waited patiently, giving me as much time as I wanted.

"I..." I cleared my throat. "I'd like to choose."

"Of course. You'll have to put something on to go into the market, though. My warning about killing anyone who sees your breasts still stands." His voice was back to playful, despite his threat.

Honestly, his threat didn't offend me in the slightest. It made me feel sort of loved.

And that was a very, very foreign feeling for me.

"Okay." I held a hand through the tent flap, and the same bag from earlier was placed in it. Pulling the bag back inside, I tried not to look at the color of the undergarment or dress as I pulled them both on. The white was bright, and made me uncomfortable, but the fabric was soft and stretchy. Namir was right about it feeling good on my skin.

I caught myself hoping that I'd find black and gold clothing of the same quality as the white and silver I was putting on, though I knew that wasn't important. What mattered was finding clothing that didn't remind me of the bastards who had hurt me so many times, for so many years.

I slipped out of the tent, smoothing the fabric down my abdomen. I felt a bit bloated—a consequence of the incredible meals the king had been feeding me, I supposed. Whether or not I looked as bloated as I felt, I didn't care. I'd survived a nightmarish childhood; the opinions of those who hadn't been through my hell mattered little to me.

Namir's eyes slowly trailed down my body, smoldering a bit as they widened. "I should've told her to pick more conservative clothing," he mumbled to himself.

I frowned, looking down at my body. "Does it look bad?"

A rough chuckle escaped him. "Not in the fucking slightest, Love." He held a wide-toothed comb toward me. "I'm just going to be snarling at other men like a rabid wolf for a bit."

The wolf thing hit me a bit hard, and my eyes narrowed toward him a bit.

"It's the bond," he explained quickly. "Having the eyes of others on you makes me feel as if I need to piss on my territory—and you're my territory."

A snort escaped me. "Refrain yourself then, *Love*." I turned his pet name back on him, and earned a playful grin for it.

"I won't make any promises."

I shook my head at him as I started down the trail of sorts that Namir and his friends had begun making as they moved back and forth from the town to the forest. The comb worked better than my fingers ever had when it came to detangling my hair, and I barely noticed the tugs and yanks as I worked through the knots.

When I'd finished, I glanced down at my dress, searching for a place to put the comb. There were no pockets—why did women's dresses not have pockets? Everyone had shit to carry, if just snacks.

"Here." Namir offered a hand.

The prisoner in me tightened my fingers around the comb. Giving back something I had been given, something that was useful, that I needed, felt absolutely insane.

But I *did* trust Namir.

Mostly.

And I wasn't chained anymore, despite my struggle with my emotions and everything else.

I slowly peeled my fingers off the comb, and then handed it to the king. He tucked it into his pants' pocket—damned reasonable men's clothing.

My fingers lifted to my hair, and I struggled to wrestle the strands into a braid while also walking. It turned out strange-looking, and loose, and I didn't have anything to wrap around the end—dammit.

Huffing, I stopped walking and reached up to the nearest tree, grabbing a long, thin leaf as the braid unraveled itself without me holding it together.

"I can do it, if you'll let me," Namir offered, leaning up against a tree. "I used to have long hair, years ago. I can braid well."

I scowled at him. "I want to be able to do it myself."

He nodded. "We can buy some fabric in the market, so you can practice more easily. This time, I could do it for you."

That... wasn't a terrible suggestion.

He was offering to teach me, I thought. Or at least to make it easier for me to learn.

Though my pride disagreed, I reluctantly nodded, turning my back to him. I assumed his braid would start at the base of my neck, like the ones Akari had taught me. But instead, he deftly gathered a small bit of hair from the top of my head, and parted it into three. His fingers moved rapidly but gently as he added bits of hair, moving down my head as he went. He was only working on one side of my head, but when he got to the ends of it, he fished a hair tie from his pocket and pulled it out to finish off the braid.

"Lavee is good with hair. We could stop by the castle one day, and she could trim the ends of yours, if you'd like. It wouldn't tangle as easily if she did, so it would be more manageable for you," he explained, as he began a second braid.

Akari had told me that people usually got their hair cut every few months—that it kept their hair healthier, and softer.

"Does my hair feel gross?" I asked him, abruptly.

"Not in the slightest." He didn't hesitate with that answer.

"You'd better not be lying to me," I warned.

He chuckled. "You thanked me for my honesty in the forest, Diora. Clearly, honesty is important to you, so I haven't lied to you. And I won't."

That made my shoulders relax slightly. "But my hair would be softer if I got it cut?"

"A bit. If you want to make it softer, you'll need to use shampoo and conditioner. Have you heard of them?"

The words were strange, but I forced myself to try to recall them. I finally shook my head a bit. "No."

"Shampoo is a soap that cleans dirt and grease from hair. Conditioner is a combination of oils and other things that you let sit on the strands, to soften and smooth them," he explained. There was no judgment behind his explanation; I didn't think he thought less of me for not knowing what they were.

"Oh." I bit my lip a bit. There were many things I didn't know about—and I wanted to learn all of them, but doing so while I was living in the forest wasn't exactly going to be easy.

Namir had offered to let me live in the castle, but I had been afraid, then. I was still afraid, but now I trusted him a bit. And... I didn't want to live in the forest.

I didn't want to ask him to let me live in his castle either, though. My pride wasn't *completely* destroyed.

I decided I'd ask if we could stop there and look at the castle after I picked a dress out, and maybe he would invite me to live there again while we were looking.

Namir finished the second braid, and tied it off with another tie he pulled from his pocket. I didn't ask how he'd known he'd need them—he had seen the state of my hair before, and it had been an absolute wreck.

We continued walking, and Namir's hands slipped into the pockets of his pants as we went. We were quiet, mostly, and the forest was peaceful. The stars glittered above us, the crescent moon shining as it always did.

"How many coins do we have?" I asked him, as we approached the edge of the town.

"None. The people in my court won't charge me; I fund their businesses with money from my family's pockets if there are expenses they can't cover and bills they can't pay."

The words surprised me.

I would definitely only choose one dress and undergarment, if they weren't going to charge me. I only needed one; I could wash it at nights, and dry it while I slept, as I had in the inns on my way to Namir's city.

"I can tell that they love you," I remarked, as we stepped out of the trees and up to the edge of one of the city's soft, dark, packed-dirt roads. "You're a good king."

"I try." Namir shrugged. "Much of my time and energy goes toward trying to take my brother out."

The words turned my stomach.

"You still want me to kill him, don't you?"

He shook his head, flashing me a serious look. "I didn't know what you'd been through, then, and was struck silly by the way you looked at me—and attacked me. I don't want you to do anything you'll regret, and something tells me that you would regret killing one of my brothers."

My stomach tensed.

He had no idea how accurate his assumption was, or how heavy the regret for ending the lives I'd already taken was. I'd killed those people in self-defense, but that didn't mean I felt right about it.

So I nodded, and said nothing else.

CHAPTER 10

THE CROWD GREW louder as we approached the market, and I heard people both whispering and calling out Namir's name, along with the word, "Mate."

I started to feel overwhelmed by the attention we received, and my monster threatened to force her way out, to consume me.

Namir seemed to realize I was struggling, because his hand slipped around mine. He held my palm to his, flashing me a small, supportive smile. He leaned in, murmuring, "My shadows can keep you calm."

My stomach loosened a bit, and my shoulders relaxed as his magic swirled over my arm, dancing slowly and lightly up my skin. The contact made bumps break out over my arms, but it relaxed the monster within me too, so I held on to Namir like my life depended on it.

And though my life didn't technically depend on it, those of the people in the market did.

They were careful not to jostle us as we walked, giving us space as we wandered. Namir seemed to know where he was going, but stopped a few times to taste foods people offered him. After he tasted a small bite of each of the foods, he handed the rest to me—ensuring me that they were safe, and sharing the food with a wink.

I found myself feeling just a bit happier every time he offered me his food, and the more we walked, I found myself having more fun as well.

People surprised me by offering silver jewelry and clothing items, but they stayed far enough away that Namir could respectfully turn them down, explaining, "Diora prefers gold."

They were all surprised by that.

None of the wealthier merchants seemed to have anything in gold at all, which made things easier, because I didn't want to take their items without coins to trade anyway.

Eventually, we made it toward the less-wealthy portion of the marketplace. The people there were even more generous, bringing so much food that Namir needed a bag to hold it all, and paper to wrap it in to preserve it a bit longer. He continued grinning at the fae, thanking them. Though his grin was genuine, it wasn't the same grin he gave me—and I wondered why.

The people were more energetic in the poorer section (their black clothes and gold jewelry gave them away), and none of them wore anything with holes. None of them were scarred, or anywhere near as skinny as I was, either—I stood out in that way, I supposed.

Overall, the people seemed to be very well taken-care-of, and the way they loved Namir was clear. He was a good king, and a kind and generous one too.

If he hadn't already had my trust, he certainly did after I saw the way his people looked up to him.

We stopped in front of the stall of a woman with dark skin who had two racks of black dresses behind her. She beamed at Namir, and took his hand between both of hers. There was no physical way to tell a fae's age, since we were damn near immortal, so I had no way to know what her relationship was with Namir.

And the way she grabbed his hand did not sit well with me.

At all.

My gaze narrowed in on the place she held his hand.

Namir glanced over at me when my body stiffened, and his shadows thickened over my hand and arm when my magic gathered within my chest.

Possessiveness; it had to be possessiveness that my monster was reacting to.

But why was she reacting to that?

"It's good to see you, Halla. I'm afraid Diora here is my mate, so I'm going to need my hand back." He winked at her, and she sighed happily as she released him.

"I've so hoped you'd find her."

"As did I." He squeezed our combined hands lightly. "Where's your mate today?"

He caught my attention with that one, and I looked over at him with interest.

"Oh, the old bastard's out hunting for more of my favorite fruits again." She rolled her eyes, though there was a fond smile on her face. "He'll start to miss me in an hour or two and come running home empty-handed."

Namir chuckled, and I finally looked at the woman. My eyes narrowed in on her throat, and widened as I followed the strange markings over her skin.

I'd forgotten about that part of the connection, in my tent earlier.

As the bond developed, markings in a lost, ancient language would slowly appear on the pair of fated mates' skin in the shimmering gold of magic that none of us could possess or change.

This woman, Halla, had found her fated mate and chosen to bond with him.

Stars, there were so many questions I'd like to ask her.

But if Namir was close with her, maybe he already knew the answer to those questions.

"Diora prefers black and gold," Namir explained, catching my attention again. "We were hoping you could help her out."

I thought I might've missed some part of the conversation, but had no desire to announce my distraction out loud.

"We'll bring coins afterward," I added hastily, not wanting her to think I was hoping she would just hand over her wares without any financial gain.

"Oh, nonsense. The king's fated doesn't pay here." She waved it off, then gestured me back behind her stall. "Let me see what I have that will fit you. I'll need to measure your hips, waist, and bust."

I released Namir's hand, assuming he would stay close. He hadn't wandered away even when I'd tried to force him to thus far, so I couldn't imagine he'd choose that moment to leave me.

Halla pulled out a long strip of fabric with lines on it, and I eyed it suspiciously.

Noticing me staring, she frowned a bit. "This is just a measuring tape. It goes around you, to tell me how wide you are."

Ah.

I nodded, like I'd known from the beginning. The last thing I wanted was for everyone in the city to know that I was clueless about so many things.

She circled me, quickly wrapping her measuring tape around me in a few different locations. My eyebrows lifted when it went around the middle of my breasts, but she was moving it somewhere else before I could feel violated.

"Do you know your height?" She continued measuring.

I looked at Namir.

"No. She's had... an interesting life," he explained without actually explaining anything.

"I've never seen measurements like these before. You haven't been feeding her enough," Halla tsked at the king, stretching her tape from the top of my head to my toes. "I'll have to alter something."

My face heated. "You don't need to do that. I—"

"I spent five years locked in the Dark King's dungeon, dear, and my wrists don't look like that," Halla said bluntly, gesturing toward the scars around mine.

My face flushed further.

"You've had a hard life, and that's nothing to be ashamed of, but things will change here. Namir is a good king, and a better man. He takes care of us, and we take care of him as much as we can in response—and you, my dear, are a part of him now. So we're going to take care of you, whether you like it or not." Her words were blunt, but I didn't hate them.

I didn't hate them at all.

"I have bracelets as well, if you wish to cover your scars." She gestured to my wrists again, and my stomach clenched.

"No. I won't hide the proof of my survival; I lived through things most fae can't even imagine, and I'm proud of that," I said, my voice sharp.

"As you should be." She led me back to Namir, and he recaptured my hand as soon as I was within his reach. "I'll have the dress and undergarment to the castle first thing in the morning," Halla explained, scribbling a few notes down on a sheet of thick paper. "Would you mind if I gave your measurements to a few other seamstresses who wish to make you something?" She looked to me.

I looked to Namir.

He shrugged.

Guess it was up to me.

"That's fine. I don't have coins yet, though."

She waved a hand through the air. "I told you, we'll take care of you."

"Thank you." Honestly, I wasn't sure whether to be shocked, suspicious, or touched by her generosity.

Namir and I made our way through the rest of the market, stopping a few more times for food and other small trinkets. By the time we made it through and walked back toward the castle, I was exhausted. The moon was nearly lost in the sky, yet we took the long way through the city, past buildings with large windows and massive skylights.

When we finally neared the castle, I wanted nothing more than to drop to the ground.

Namir wanted to leave some of the food we'd been given in the castle, so it didn't go to waste, but I'd decided I was abandoning my plan to slyly convince him to invite me to live there again.

I didn't want to go back out to the forest, where it was cold and dirty. I wanted a warm bed, and a warm meal, and a set of sturdy walls around me.

"Does your offer to give me a room here still stand?" I asked Namir bluntly.

"Of course." He looked surprised by the question. "The rooms are large, and sometimes cold, though."

My face fell.

"But they have lights; we can leave them on, so it's not dark while you sleep, if that would work," he added. "And my room has a glass ceiling, so you can see the stars. It's yours, if you want it."

I scowled at him. "I'm not taking your room."

His lips twitched. "I'd take the floor, if you forced me to."

I heaved a sigh.

Maybe this was a bad idea.

"Come on; I'll help you pick out a room that *doesn't* belong
to me." He tugged me toward the castle. My feet dragged,
but I let him pull me behind him.

The castle was even more beautiful to me the second time,
because the second time, there was no one seated on the
furniture within it. The absence of the other fae was more
comfortable to me.

"The only people who live here are those I'm the closest to,"
Namir explained, leading me toward a set of gray doors I
hadn't noticed before, tucked beneath the massive staircase.
"They all live on the top floor; this portion of the castle is
mine. I don't mind company, but no one enters my rooms.
They know that's where I draw the line. And, I have the
shadows attuned to my magic alone, so they can't get in." He
winked at me as he placed his hand on the doors.

My eyebrows shot upward as the doors turned to shadow and
faded in the center, creating a gap large enough for a fae to fit
through.

"I hope you don't intend to kill me in here," I grumbled at
him, as he led me inside first with a hand at my lower back.

He laughed. "Maybe after we take my brothers out and I get
my magic back."

I heard the tease in his voice, and knew he was joking. My lips curved upward slightly for the tiniest moment, but my small smile had disappeared by the time Namir caught up to me. I looked around as we stopped walking, and the doors reformed behind us.

Namir's portion of the castle was made of the same stone as the rest of it, and was wide and open. Off to my right was a monstrously large bed, with a rectangular sheet of glass in the ceiling above it as he'd told me there was. It would be nice to sleep beneath the stars, while also safely enclosed.

The rest of his space held couches, bookshelves, and a large kitchen.

Did the Shadow King cook?

Did he read?

I didn't ask him, though I was curious.

"I thought you were giving me an empty room." I looked at him. "I'm not stealing yours."

He raised a hand up beside his head, as if surrendering. "It was worth a try."

I rolled my eyes, and his lips twitched like he was fighting a grin.

"Come on, Love. I'll show you the available rooms."

CHAPTER 11

NAMIR SHOWED me all three of the open rooms. None of them were ideal, honestly, each of them sandwiched between other people's rooms. They each had their own bathroom, though, and I was definitely not opposed to the idea of taking showers again instead of bathing in the stream like I had in the forest.

I finally picked the one closest to the stairs.

Namir set the bags of extra food down in my room, near the door. He told me to let him know if I needed anything, and then flashed me a grin before I shut the door behind myself.

I knew it wouldn't be hard to find him if I did need anything —he'd be in his room. Other people couldn't get through his shadows, but I'd never had a problem doing so.

Turning on all of the lights in the room, bathroom, and closet, I wandered the space to check it all out. It was simple, but beautiful. The walls and flooring were made of the same shadow-infused-looking stone that the castle was crafted out of, and as I walked, the stone seemed to darken beneath my feet, like the shadows within were gathering to greet me.

There was a large bathroom, with a door to separate it from the rest of the space. It had a toilet that flushed, and a huge shower, as well as a bathtub. Akari had explained bathtubs to me years earlier, but I'd always found the idea of sitting in a tub of my own filth to be disgusting.

Outside the bathroom, I found the entrance to the closet. It was almost as big as the bathroom, a huge walk-in space with strange cylindrical rods protruding from the walls at a little above my height.

I ran my fingers over them, feeling the smooth stone they were also crafted out of. The whole castle was a masterpiece, as far as I'd seen, and I wasn't sure whether to feel lucky or intimidated by being there.

It was too late to go back to the forest now, though, and truthfully, I didn't want to.

I slipped out of the white and silver dress I'd been wearing—and had tried not to pay too much attention to. After dropping that and the undergarment I'd had on beneath it in the closet, I padded into the bathroom. The bed was huge and looked extremely comfortable, and I didn't want to ruin it with the dirt that remained on my skin from so much time in the forest.

The shower functioned similarly to the ones in the inns I'd stayed at, so I twisted the lever to turn it on. At the inns, the water had come out cold at first. Because of that, I dodged the stream as both shower heads above me began to rain. Then I tested the water with a hand, found it already warm, and I slipped beneath it.

It took me a few minutes to get the water to a temperature I liked, but then I grabbed the brand-new bar of soap off one of the shelves to the side of the shower, and began scrubbing with it.

I was surprised—and disgusted—by the amount of dirt that stained the water as it ran down my skin and into the drain under my feet.

When the water finally ran clear, I turned my attention to the two bottles of soap on the shelf above the one that I set my bar of soap back down on.

I assumed the bottles held the hair soaps Namir had told me about; shampoo, and conditioner. The first would strip the oils and dirt from my hair, the second would soften it. There were labels on the bottles, but I couldn't read, so that didn't help me.

After undoing the complex braids Namir had done in my hair, I grabbed one of the bottles and tested a dab of the soap from within it on the ends of my hair, checking to see what it did. When my hair felt soft and slippery with the creamy solution on it, I decided it was probably conditioner, and rinsed it out.

I grabbed the first one, and squirted it into my palm before lifting my hands to my hair.

It was definitely removing the dirt, I decided, as the water once again ran brown. I tried not to let myself feel disgusted by that, given that I'd used soap on the strands back in the inns I'd stayed at. I had been clean before; I'd just lived in the forest for a bit.

That was over, though.

I had a... well, not a home, I supposed. A temporary living space. Or maybe a temporary *home*.

It struck me, as I washed my hair again, and again, that Namir and I weren't temporary. Even if I left his castle, even when I went back out to the inn to find my friends, he and I would be fated. And if our bond continued to grow, there would be evidence of that on my throat, magically engraved into my skin.

I wasn't sure whether I was unsettled by that, or calmed by it. My emotions were too difficult to read.

But my magic wasn't gathering, my monster remaining dormant in my chest, so I at least didn't feel in danger because of it.

When my hair was finally free of dirt, I slathered it in the conditioner. I'd noticed a wide-toothed comb resting on another shelf above the shampoo, so I grabbed that and ran it through my hair as the creamy solution sat on the strands, soaking them and softening them. They were much easier to detangle than they had ever been before, and surprise flooded me as it slid through my hair like it was silk.

I wasn't sure how long I was supposed to leave the conditioner in, so I just continued combing it for a while, leaning up against the wall while the water ran over my legs and chest. It was warm, and comfortable, and nice. I wasn't sure I'd ever felt so relaxed in my life.

When I grew tired of standing and decided I was ready to sleep, I set the comb back in its place and rinsed the conditioner from my hair, musing to myself in shock as I realized the strands were now just as soft and smooth without the conditioner in as they had been with it in.

Annoyance had my jaw clenching.

Namir must've been lying to me in the forest; my hair had felt scratchy, then, and he was used to feeling smooth hair, softened and detangled by conditioner.

I shut the water off and looked for a towel. The closest thing I found to that was a large, white robe. It had arm holes, so I shoved my arms through and awkwardly used the thick, soft fabric to dry my body. My hair was still dripping wet, so I clumsily braided it back—still musing about the softness, and pissed with Namir for his lie—and squeezed as much water out of the thick rope of it as I could manage.

My mood was fouled, but I tried not to let that prevent me from enjoying the space I now occupied.

I left the bathroom and closet doors open and lights on, crossing the room to turn off the one over the main area. When it was off, I gave my eyes a moment to adjust before I determined whether or not I could sleep like that.

The lights in the closet and bathroom were bright, and they illuminated the space enough that I could still see everything decently well. So, I headed toward the bed, determined to get a good night's sleep away from Namir just to spite the bastard for lying to me.

I slipped into the bed and closed my eyes, marveling silently about the thick cushion beneath my back. It was just firm enough and just soft enough to hold me in place while still conforming to my shape. The feel of it was incredible, especially when paired with the thick, soft blankets cuddling me from above.

Sleep whisked me away quickly, and for the first time in my life, I dreamed.

A NOISE in the hallway dragged me from the strange dream I'd been living in, filled with black dresses and gold jewelry. The silk had been so soft that I'd nearly been able to feel it against my skin, despite knowing it wasn't real.

The whole thing was disorienting, but strangely pleasurable too.

I heard a muffled voice outside. It was familiar, but I couldn't make out the words or determine the gender of the person speaking.

A soft chuckle that I most definitely did recognize sent bumps over my skin—and fury coursing through me.

Namir was outside, laughing with someone.

Namir, who had lied to me about liking the feel of my hair.

Namir, who had claimed to have saved himself for his mate —for me.

What if he was out there with a woman?

What if he was flirting with her, or attracted to her? What if she could read, and write, and function in normal society? What if she wasn't scarred, and smiled constantly, and laughed just as frequently as he did?

My stomach was clenched so tightly I nearly couldn't breathe.

I threw my legs out of the bed, nearly falling over before I righted myself and stalked across the room. Flinging the door open, I prepared myself for a verbal sparring—and found myself face-to-face with Jesh, of all people.

Namir was sitting on his ass on the floor, his back resting where the closed door had been a moment before.

Most of my anger vanished.

Not all, but most.

"Goodnight," Jesh said, his voice gruff and clipped as he strode down the hall like something had bitten him on the ass.

"What are you doing out here?" I snarled at Namir, forcing myself to remember why I was furious.

"Why are you naked?" He stood swiftly, his voice a growl as he put a hand on my bare abdomen and used it to propel me back into my room.

I glanced down at my body—right.

Naked.

"I'm not used to wearing clothes constantly—and you didn't answer my question." I forced my voice to grow angry again. "What the hell were you doing sitting outside my room?"

Those gorgeous gray eyes of his swirled with emotions—possessiveness, and something deeper, and hotter, that I couldn't name.

"The same thing I was doing with you in the forest. Protecting you." His growl faded, his tone growing silkier. "Stars, Diora, do you have no idea how you affect me? It's a damn good thing Jesh made a run for it—I still feel the urge to grab him by the throat and acquaint his face with my fist until he's forgotten how sexy you look bare like this."

I blinked at him, his words catching me completely and totally off-guard. "I thought he was a woman. I heard you laugh. There was no thinking involved—I just reacted."

Namir stepped closer. His hand was gentle as it caught my arm, cradling my elbow. "There's no other woman for me, Love. There never has been, and there never will be. I'm yours, as much as you're mine. Which is why you'll never answer the damned door naked again. Understand?" His voice remained silky, still, and that made my body react strangely—my lower belly tightening, and my flesh warming.

Was that lust?

Akari had tried to explain it to me years earlier, but it hadn't made any sense to me at the time.

"Fine," I said, my voice clipped. "You're not staying outside my door all night, though. Go back to your room."

His lips curved upward playfully. "The only way I'm going back to my room is if you go with me."

I scowled. "Not a chance."

He released my elbow and gave me a quick bow, his smile morphing into a teasing grin. "Then if you'll excuse me, there's a strip of tile calling my ass back."

Namir made it to the door before I growled, "I don't want you sleeping out there. What if another woman *does* walk by?"

He chuckled, continuing out. "Then she'll see a devoted male sleeping outside his female's room, keeping her safe." He tugged the door open, and I crossed the room, catching it before he closed it.

Quickly, he turned so he blocked the doorway with his gigantic body. Anyone who walked past would see his bare back—not my naked figure.

His playful grin remained in place even as his jaw clenched a bit. "What did I say about the nudity, Love? You're more than welcome to strip yourself bare for me any time you'd like, but not while others can see—this is mine." He gestured a hand toward me, sweeping it up and down.

My scowl deepened, and I growled back, "I am *not* yours, Namir. And you are *not* sleeping in the hallway. Get your stubborn ass in the room and close the damn door."

His eyebrows lifted, but he did as I'd commanded, stepping inside smoothly and closing the door as he did so. Our bare chests brushed before I took a step back too, and a shudder ravaged me in response to the touch.

Fuck, was *that* lust?

Holy hell, that was strong.

"You haven't showered," I told him, my voice flat. He had still lied to me—and even if what I was feeling was lust, I wasn't ready to explore it. Not in the slightest.

"I don't need a shower to sleep on the floor, Diora." His voice was back to playful, but it seemed to have faded a bit. His playfulness usually seemed genuine, but now there was something about it that seemed a bit... faded.

Was it just a front?

Was he using his playfulness to hide his emotions from me?

I scoffed. "You're a damned king, you're not sleeping on the floor. Go take a shower, and we'll share a bed. I don't want your dirt on the blankets—and we don't need to snuggle for warmth this time."

I strode back to my bed, my body thrumming with a feeling I'd determined had to be lust. What else could the damned discomfort be?

Namir's eyes tracked me to the bed, but he finally stepped into the bathroom. He didn't close the door behind him, but I didn't watch him strip—my apparent lustiness sure as hell didn't need the assistance of that mental image.

I closed my eyes and tried to fall asleep, but this time, the sleep didn't come.

CHAPTER 12

I TRIED to toss and turn silently, so Namir wouldn't hear. My brain kept trying to come up with what the bastard might look like in that shower, naked and wet, but I'd never seen him without his clothes on. And since I'd never seen any other man naked, either, my imagination had nothing to work with.

When the shower shut off, I flopped to my stomach and tried to ignore the curiosity tugging at me to roll over and get an eyeful of Namir's naked body. He'd seen me bare a few times already, but never on purpose on either of our parts.

I was a bit sweaty beneath the blankets, that infuriating lust making my lower belly ache. I didn't even know what I was lusting for, other than that Namir definitely had it. It pissed me off, but I tried to ignore that too, because I sure as the stars wasn't doing anything about it that night.

My eyes were closed, and I acted as if I was asleep when I heard Namir's footsteps on the stone floor. They were quiet, but not so quiet that my overactive mind couldn't keep up. I knew he didn't have any clean clothing, and I'd been clear when I told him I didn't want his dirt in my bed, so it was safe to assume that he would slip beneath the blankets with me just as naked as I was.

And that only made my body clench harder, in more frustration.

I was used to pain and discomfort, but this was something else entirely.

Not pain, but a severe discomfort different than any I'd ever experienced.

The bed didn't dip as Namir rustled the blankets. I heard a quiet groan when the blankets moved down my back a bit, flashing a bit of my bare ass, but the king didn't do anything about it.

Instead, he tugged the blankets back up, and got comfortable on the empty side of the bed. The mattress was plenty large enough for both of us, despite his massive size.

After a few long moments of me still pretending to be asleep while struggling to control my damned lust, I felt a brush of Namir's shadows on my bare arm.

The tension in my lower belly relaxed instantly, and I began to breathe deeply again.

My shadows reacted to his, and I heard a soft sigh from Namir's side of the bed. Our magic would make sharing space a bit easier, I supposed.

His shadows continued to slip over my skin, and eventually, I managed to fall back asleep.

When I woke the next morning, I felt completely disoriented.

Wrestling my eyes open, I forced myself to look at my surroundings—and found myself staring at Namir's neck and muscular shoulder.

I was definitely still on my side of the bed—but he was most certainly not.

At some point during the night, I'd rolled to my back, and he'd rolled on top of me. His body was draped over mine, his chin tucked against my neck and shoulder while his forehead was against a pillow. One of his arms was draped over the mattress, the other buried under the pillow we were both laying on. And his legs—fuck, his legs.

One had been slung over me, just far enough that his erection was nestled between my thighs, a little above my knees.

My entire body nearly burst into flames at the feel of his hardness there.

I needed an out.

A fast, fast out.

But... how? The man weighed an assload, and was very securely wrapped around me. He hated mornings—and his rhythmic snores reassured me that he was still very much asleep. There wasn't a chance in hell that I could roll away from him.

And what options did that leave me?

Magic.

Namir had turned completely to shadow before. My monster had done it when I escaped my prison, too, so I knew I could also do it.

I would just need to focus.

The king's magic lesson came to mind.

"See it like a hand, and it'll move like a hand. Your magic is an extension of your body."

Theoretically, I could see my magic as engulfing me, turning me to shadows, and it would happen. It had worked when I did so with my hand in the forest, right?

Swallowing an assload of stress and fear, I looked down at my bare arms, and imagined them becoming shadow. It took a lot of focus, but the shadow slowly engulfed my skin, taking over completely.

I focused more, my forehead knitting as I urged the shadows to continue moving down more of my body, to spread and cover me.

Finally, they did, and I focused on seeing them turn to mist.

The moment I saw it in my mind, Namir's body fell *through* my shadows. He kept snoring—didn't even notice the change.

But I rolled off the bed, dropping the magic as soon as I was free of the king's massive form.

My breathing was quick, my chest rising and falling rapidly as my body relaxed.

I had done it.

I had formed my magic exactly how I wanted to—and used it to break free.

A soft, breathless laugh escaped me, but Namir continued right on snoring.

I wasn't weak.

I wasn't trapped.

I was powerful, and free.

...so long as my monster didn't rip control away from me again soon.

My stomach rumbled, but I had no desire to wake Namir. He was a grouch in the mornings, and then he'd see me naked again, which would cause all sorts of awkwardness and lust on my part. And I'd probably see him naked too, which would only encourage the annoying lust that had begun developing the night before.

So I slipped into the closet silently. Grimacing at the white and silver fabric, I pulled the dirty underclothing and dress over my skin, setting it properly into place. Halla would be dropping off my new clothes a bit later, so I would put them on when they got there—after I showered again, of course. I wouldn't want to ruin my new clothes.

I slipped out of my room and headed down the hallway to find food, unraveling my braid as I went. My hair was still slightly damp, and so incredibly soft that I found myself petting it a bit. I knew I was strange, but I couldn't stop myself—it had never felt so smooth before.

I passed a few people I didn't recognize as I headed down the stairs. Most of them gawked at me, so I ignored them.

Stress clenched my stomach a bit, but I forced myself to remain standing straight. I was a survivor; their judgmental stares weren't going to change that.

I found the castle's kitchen and dining room off to the side of the staircase, through another door that I hadn't noticed the first time I was in the castle. Everything was built out of the same shadowy stone, which made it difficult to tell things apart sometimes.

There were a handful of tables and chairs spread out in the part of the wide room nearest to me, and a few male and female fae cooking up a storm in a huge kitchen behind them. I stopped just inside the doorway, and watched in fascination.

I didn't know how to cook—I might like to learn that. To do so, I'd need a kitchen and a teacher, though. Maybe one of the fae in there would teach me.

"Does Namir know you're down here?" Jesh's voice rumbled behind me.

I spun around swiftly, smacking him in the chest with my hair, much to his apparent amusement.

"Easy." He held up a hand. "I mean no harm."

"Namir's sleeping. He's a miserable bastard in the mornings." My voice was clipped; Jesh and I were not friends. He had broken my trust moments after we met.

Jesh lifted an eyebrow. "And you think leaving your room without him will make him *less* of a miserable bastard?"

I shrugged. "I'm hungry, and I want to learn how to cook."

Spinning away from Jesh, I fought a snort as my hair whacked him in the chest again before I strode toward the kitchen.

The fae would probably turn me down when I asked them to teach me, but it couldn't hurt to ask, could it? Namir was the king, and whether or not he was a miserable bastard, he wouldn't let them attack me. And even if they did, my shadowed monster would fight back, harder.

There seemed to be some kind of a line to get food, so I fell into place at the back of it, waiting until the line moved closer to the fae. I didn't grab a plate for myself—I wanted to cook food on my own, not eat theirs.

"Excuse me?" I called out, as I neared one of the fae cooking. The man glanced up at me, his expression one of surprise. "Excuse me," I called again, remaining in place even as the rest of the line continued moving.

He pointed to himself, and I nodded vigorously.

Setting down the huge bowl he was stirring something in, he crossed the distance between us and stopped behind the countertop separating us, resting his large hands on the marbled stone.

"Can you teach me to cook?" I asked him.

He blinked.

Shit.

He didn't want to teach me.

I shouldn't have asked.

My stomach clenched a bit. "It's alright if you can't. I know my magic's not well controlled, and most people are probably a bit afraid of me. I... uh..." I stepped back. "Sorry."

The room grew silent, everyone stilling.

Stars.

They were all staring at me, weren't they?

My magic gathered in my stomach, and I tried frantically to shove it down, to calm it.

I should never have—

"What the fuck is going on here?" Namir's snarl made me jump, but his hand landed on my shoulder, and my magic dissolved in my abdomen. He had my damned shadows practically trained.

"Nothing," I said stiffly.

"You left me in bed alone, for nothing?" His growl made my throat swell a bit.

What was I supposed to say?

Everyone was still staring at us.

"Do you even have food?" He turned, and must've noticed Jesh sitting nearby, because he snarled at his friend, "Why has she not been fed?"

I scowled at the way he spoke about me like I was incapable of taking care of myself.

"She didn't come looking for food. She wants to learn how to cook," Jesh drawled.

There was a beat of silence.

Namir finally sighed, "Dammit. Sorry, everyone. I'll work on controlling my temper."

Snorts went around the room; apparently it was common knowledge that the king was a grumpy asshole in the morning.

He tugged me backward just a bit, and the food line resumed its motion as he spun me around to face him.

I glared at him. "I was handling it."

His eyes softened, his lips curling up slightly. "I know you were."

The words diffused my anger immediately.

Did the man realize how good he was at that? Calming me down?

Stars, I hoped not.

His fingers slid over the back of my neck, making me shiver a bit as he touched my skin lightly. I expected to hate the feeling, but I loved it.

His voice lowered, his head tilting down so it nearly touched mine, and his lips almost brushing mine as he murmured, "Don't leave me while I'm sleeping unless you want me to wake up and murder someone, Diora. I thought you'd left me, or been taken from me."

My mind blanked at the words.

How was I supposed to growl at him for saying sweet shit like that?

"I'd like to get you a plate of food, Love. Is that alright?"

Damn, he was being way too nice.

"Fine," I huffed half-heartedly.

His lips curved further upward, and he murmured a soft, "thank you," before releasing me.

I dropped into a chair across from Jesh's at a round, five-chair table, and my gaze tracked Namir.

He stepped into line behind the last fae, not asking for or expecting special treatment. No one tried to start a conversation with him, probably expecting him to be his normal grumpy-morning self. But a few of them flashed him smiles or waved, and he responded with small smiles.

That made me more jealous than I wanted to admit.

His white pants were wrinkled and dirty, his hair was wild, and his face showed clear signs of exhaustion.

Had I really worried him?

CHAPTER 13

MY GAZE LEFT Namir after a few moments, and lifted back to the people in the kitchen, growing wistful.

I shouldn't have expected them to want to teach me. I had done terrible things in their city—I had lost control of my magic, and hurt people, after I attempted to kill the king they clearly loved.

But I still wanted to learn to cook.

I didn't have any useful skills or any experience in trades. All I knew was torture, and survival, and fear, and misery.

But things were different, now that I'd escaped my captors. And I wanted to be different, too. I wanted to learn to cook, maybe to sew too. Anything that wasn't violent, or painful. I'd done so much harm already, and survived so much pain, that I wanted to do something creative. I wanted to improve the world, not worsen it.

My eyes were still on the fae in the kitchen, my mind still churning through the small list of things I already knew I wanted to try with my newfound freedom. Namir had wanted to teach me to fight, but I didn't want any more violence in my life.

Now that I had some freedom, like my friend Vena, I wanted peace.

Namir dropped into the seat beside mine, setting a plate in front of me that was even fuller than the one he set in front of himself.

As soon as Namir sat, Jesh made his way to the food line. It occurred to me that he had remained beside me until Namir was there—either to keep me safe, or to make the king happy. Or maybe both, I guessed.

Namir and I ate in silence, but the sides of our feet remained touching, our shadows slipping off our skin and sort of dancing together in the space between our bodies, so it was a comfortable silence. The king really did look exhausted, and I couldn't help but feel a bit bad for that. He had treated me well, and I probably shouldn't have abandoned him in bed, stressing him out further.

Namir cleared his plate, and then leaned back in his seat and watched me. When I stopped before I'd cleared my own plate, my abdomen too swollen to eat another bite, he nudged my foot with his. "Keep eating."

I scowled at him. "I'm stuffed."

His expression was soft, but not playful this time. "I want you healthy, Love. I could still see your ribs last night."

Last night...

When I had answered the door naked.

My face heated a bit, and I growled back, "Maybe I like looking like that."

I didn't.

Really, I didn't care all that much how I looked. But I didn't want to look sickly, or tortured, or unhealthy.

"You look fucking incredible." He didn't so much as hesitate with those words, and that made me bite my lip to hide a small, irrational smile. "But I want you to *feel* incredible."

My heart squeezed.

Damn him.

A sigh escaped me. "I really can't eat anymore, or I'm going to puke." I slid the plate over to him, setting my fork down on it. "You don't look so hot yourself today, though, *Love*. I think you need the extra food so *you* can feel incredible."

A laugh sputtered out of him. "Stars, you're adorable." He grabbed the fork, and I noticed surprised gazes glued to us from around the room.

Yeah, yeah. He was cheerful this morning, now. Not every morning, and not because of me.

Probably.

Sort of.

Ish.

I pushed away the thought, but let my eyes linger on the gorgeous man as he worked on the food.

As Namir finished up his food, the male fae I'd spoken to earlier walked up to our table, nodding his head toward the king.

I noticed Namir's body stiffen a bit at the man's presence, but he didn't otherwise react. I didn't think the other fae noticed the king's sudden stiffness, either. I leaned a bit closer to him, hoping that would help with the possessiveness he was probably feeling—and he shocked me by setting his hand lightly on my thigh.

The contact made my throat swell, and my body flush the way it had the night before.

Holy hell, I liked the way that felt.

"You surprised me with your request earlier, Miss…" the chef trailed off.

I blinked, still caught off-guard by Namir's hand on my thigh.

"Diora," Namir offered, his voice not entirely kind.

"Miss Diora." The man inclined his head toward me. "We'd be honored to teach you how to cook."

My forehead wrinkled, and I glanced over at Namir. "Because I'm fated to him?"

"Does it matter?" The fae chef tilted his chin slightly.

I supposed it didn't.

"That would be incredible, thank you. Right now?" I glanced around the room; it was a bit full. It would probably be better for me to learn when there wasn't a crowd, honestly. I didn't exactly function well when under a lot of pressure.

"Your dresses will be delivered any time now. After you've tried them on." Namir's hand squeezed my thigh gently.

"After the breakfast rush would be perfect," the fae agreed. "We look forward to it." He gestured toward the rest of the fae in the kitchen, and hope blossomed in my abdomen.

"As do I."

The chef headed back behind the counters, getting back to work, and Namir set down the fork I hadn't realized he was still holding. His voice grew playful, and he murmured, "If you're staring at his ass, so help me, Love..."

I rolled my eyes at him, knowing that he was teasing.

Mostly teasing, at least.

His humor was a front for something more, a way to hide his emotions, I was starting to think.

"Why would you think I was staring at his ass? It's not as if I make it a habit to seek you out when you're naked, like you do to me," I shot back, hoping to get a rise out of him. As much as I loved his gentleness, I wanted to know what he was really feeling even more.

Jesh coughed on the other side of the table, and we both looked at him. "Swallowed wrong," he managed, gesturing to his throat. He looked like he was fighting a grin, though.

"Perhaps I'm wearing clothes too often," Namir drawled back, reaching down to the waistband of his pants and adjusting it a bit.

A sharp growl escaped me, and my hand clamped down on his, my head jerking as I looked around the room to make sure no one was watching him.

Everyone.

Everyone was watching him.

Him.

Me.

Us.

Wow, I was not cut out for this.

He chuckled, flashing me an amused grin as he patted my hand over his with his empty one. "Don't worry, Love. I'm all yours."

Leaning closer to me, he brushed his lips over my cheek once, and then again. It was a kiss—a soft, sweet kiss, and I had no fucking clue how I was supposed to respond to it.

So I just shot to my feet, planning an escape.

Namir caught my hand before I could leave, and his fingers slid between mine.

Stars, was that grip supposed to feel so good?

"What are you doing?" His expression was still amused.

"Going to wait for the dresses. You said they're being delivered." My voice came out harsher than I intended.

"I'll wait with you," he said easily, standing up and grabbing our plates in the hand that wasn't holding mine.

"I can handle waiting for a few dresses on my own, *Love*," I drawled his nickname for me, trying to use his accent as I said it as well.

Was my sarcasm working to cover my awkwardness?

Shit, I hoped so.

His eyes glinted with humor. "Did it occur to you that maybe *I* can't?"

It took a moment for me to process his words, and by the time I had, we were striding toward the door out of the dining room, our fingers still locked together.

Had he really just said that he couldn't handle me waiting for dresses alone?

Was the fated connection affecting him more than it was affecting me?

"What do you mean by that?" I finally asked him, all sarcasm and annoyance gone.

He flashed me a playful grin. "Maybe if you don't abandon me tomorrow morning, I'll tell you."

I scowled in response, which only made his grin widen.

We sat down in one of the couches that faced the castle's large doors.

"Do you intend to sleep in my bed every night?" I asked him, after a few moments.

"That's a good question." His words didn't sound as playful as before, and I got the feeling that he didn't know the answer to that question any more than I did. "If I said yes, would I be welcome?"

I studied the doors with far more interest than I felt. "As long as you wear pants next time, I suppose so."

He laughed. It wasn't a sarcastic laugh, or his soft chuckle, but a full-chested laugh that made me bite back a smile. "That's fair. I'd prefer if you slept naked every night, though."

I snorted. "Of course you would."

"Did I mention that your breasts are absolutely—"

The doors opened, and Halla entered, cutting the king off. I realized our hands were still connected as we stood up together.

Halla pulled the door open wider and wider, gesturing someone to follow her in. A man with markings around his throat wheeled a large metal clothing rack into the building. My eyes nearly bulged out of my head as I scanned the contents of the rack—it was overflowing with black and gold fabrics, stuffed absolutely full.

"I only wanted one dress," I whispered harshly to Namir.

He chuckled. "You may as well be my queen, Love, and if you haven't noticed, my people adore me. I'm sure this is far from the last of the gifts you'll receive from them."

My stomach clenched and my eyes opened even wider as a pair of women pushed another rack into the room, just as full as the first one.

It was just the evening before that the people had discovered what colors I preferred—how had they already created so many dresses for me?

A third rack followed the first two, and nausea turned my belly.

"I can't accept these," I whispered harshly to Namir once again, as we neared Halla, who was beaming.

"You don't have to; I will," he murmured back, his voice playful once again.

"Where should we put these?" Halla asked Namir, her voice cheerful.

Namir flashed her a grin. "We'll fit as many as we can in Diora's room, the rest will go to mine."

Another rack full of black fabric entered the castle, and I nearly vomited.

Halla smiled. "Lead the way."

Namir's shadows stroked my arm as we led the massive group up the stairs. His magic was comforting, but not nearly as comforting as I wished it would be.

The next half an hour was full of rustling fabric. I ended up seated on the edge of my bed while Namir directed everyone where to put things. More furniture was carried into the room—a large dresser, with a mirror on top of it, followed by a comfortable-looking couch.

Decorative items followed—a few small trees, one of which looked to be growing some type of fruit I didn't recognize, a few potted plants, a few painted pictures of gorgeous landscapes the likes of which I had never seen before.

It was all beautiful, but intimidating because I hadn't expected it.

Namir caught my hand again before he led me down the stairs, his shadows stroking my arm and relaxing me a bit more. There were still some more clothes hanging on the last of the rolling racks, so we'd have to stop in his room and put them away. He wouldn't allow the others in there, though, so he assured them he would carry them in himself.

We thanked most of the people and sent them on their way. Only Halla and her mate remained, waiting for the final clothing rack. They didn't have a problem mingling with a few other people who were hanging around the castle, though, and were chatting with a pair of women I didn't recognize when we left.

Namir sent me through the shadows in front of him, pulling the rack behind us. The room grew silent when the shadows closed themselves as soon as we were through, and Namir's hand found my lower back as he led me toward his closet. It was attached to the portion of the castle that his bed occupied, and when I stepped through that open door in front of him, my eyebrows shot upward.

I took the massive space in—it was at least triple the size of my own closet, and the vast majority was empty. A dozen pairs of white and silver pants hung from the cylindrical beams nearest to the door, but that was it. Otherwise, the space was empty.

"Why is your closet so large?" I asked him, as he tugged the rack in behind us.

He flashed me yet another grin. "I told you I was waiting for my fated mate. Why build a living space that wouldn't cater to her needs as well as mine?"

That was a valid point, I supposed.

"I don't need this much clothing," I said, leaning up against the doorway as he hung my things.

"My people don't gift the clothing because you need it—they gift it because they want you to have it. I'm sure there will be an uprising if you wear the same thing more than once."

My eyebrows shot upward. "You're joking, right?"

"Not in the slightest."

He lifted the white pants that had been hanging in his closet onto the now-empty rack, and I frowned. "Where are you taking your clothes?"

"They've started replacing mine too." He gestured to a pair of new pants I hadn't noticed hanging—they were black, with golden thread peeking out on the sides.

"They think we need to match?" I asked, incredulously.

He chuckled. "No. They know you prefer black and gold, and I told Halla that I wasn't going to wear white anymore. The last thing I want is to remind you of the people who mistreated you, Love."

I blinked at him. "That's... really sweet, Namir."

His grin widened. "I'm a sweet guy."

I snorted, and he winked at me.

We headed toward the door out of his room, our hands somehow finding each other again and our fingers threading together once more.

Namir tugged me toward the door, still wearing that damned sexy grin. "Come on, Diora. Let's get them their rack so they can be on their way."

CHAPTER 14

WE RETURNED the rack and thanked them again—though Namir was far more vocal with his thanks than I was. He laughed with Halla and her mate a few times before they finally left, and then it was just me and him and a castle full of people moving around, doing their own things.

"Where's Lavee today?" I asked Namir, as we headed back up the stairs to my room. I still wanted a shower, and to change my clothes. And Namir was still being stubborn about not leaving me alone.

"She does hair two days a week, to keep her skills up. At least, she claims it's to keep her skills up. I think she just likes to have a break from Jesh and I," Namir explained, his voice light and playful.

"I wouldn't blame her for that," I drawled, fighting a grin of my own.

Namir chuckled behind me as I stepped into my closet.

My gaze swept over the many new items of clothing within.

"Stars," I murmured, when my eyes caught on the section of clothes that were clearly men's. And all of them were black, gold, or black and gold.

My fingers trailed over the fabrics, and I finally selected a dress and undergarment pairing that was mostly black, with a few embroidered golden flowers along the hem and moderate round neckline. The undergarment was almost purely golden, but both were made of a buttery-soft fabric that was ridiculously light.

Namir plopped down on the foot of the bed while I slipped into the bathroom, making sure to close and lock the door behind me. He'd seen me naked a handful of times, but naked and washing myself were entirely different.

I showered quickly, careful not to get my hair wet since it had finally dried soft and wavy after being in a braid all night. When I was dried and dressed, I slipped out of the bathroom. Namir's eyes slid down me, practically burning me with his smoldering stare.

"Do you approve?" I drawled, crossing the room toward the door that would lead out.

He followed me there, catching my wrist before I could slip out. "You're breathtaking, Love. Wait for me while I shower too?"

My first instinct was to scowl at him and shoot him down, but he had really seemed a bit off-balance after I left him alone that morning.

So I gave a grudging nod. "As long as you're fast."

Relief crossed his face, and he pressed the back of my hand to his lips before he strode toward the bathroom, grabbing a pair of black pants he'd left on the foot of the bed on his way in.

I stared at my hand in surprise and confusion for far longer than I wanted to admit after the door shut behind him.

When Namir was clean and dressed in a pair of black pants that somehow made him look even more intimidating than before, we headed down the stairs. He slipped his fingers between mine, holding my hand as we walked, and my chest warmed a bit.

I stopped outside the kitchen and dining room, and Namir stopped beside me, shooting me a curious look. I bit back a sigh at the argument that I thought might follow the conversation, but I was willing to fight.

"I'd like to do this myself," I told him firmly. "I know you're feeling protective, and possessive, but I want to learn new skills and determine whether or not I enjoy this without overthinking our connection while I do so. It's nothing against you—I just want to see what it's like to learn on my own."

Namir's curious look shifted to a grimace, his jaw clenching a bit.

My body tensed.

The fight was definitely coming.

He finally let out a slow breath, and then nodded. "Alright. I'll train with Jesh and some of my other fae for as long as I can manage. It likely won't be more than a few hours."

"That's alright. And you can always just come peek in, if you need to," I said quickly, not wanting him to change his mind.

"That might help," he offered.

It sounded like a lie, but since he was lying to help me this time, I didn't mind it at all.

I was actually kind of grateful for it.

So, I flashed him a small smile. "Thanks, Namir." I turned and slipped into the kitchen, leaving him staring after me with a stunned expression on his face.

CHAPTER 15

NAMIR

"SHE SMILED AT ME," I repeated to Jesh, dodging a swing of his sword with ease. It felt like I'd had caffeine injected straight to my veins—and to my cock. "I've never seen her smile before. Have you?"

My eyes narrowed at the thought of my friend seeing my female smile before me.

"No." Jesh grunted as the blunt end of my training sword smashed him in the ribcage. "I have seen her glare at you like she wishes you were dead, though. A great many times, too."

I laughed, missing a swing of Jesh's sword. It hit me in the throat, hard, but the impact barely swayed me. That was another benefit of the throne's power that not many people knew—it made me physically stronger, and helped me heal faster than the average fae as well. I was curious if any of that power had leaked into Diora through our budding bond yet, but wasn't willing to risk scaring her off again by asking her.

"She'll come around eventually."

Jesh made a noncommittal noise. "You seem to bother her even more than most people do."

"She's not bothered, she's afraid." I swung my sword harder, and faster, letting my body take control. My magic swirled off my skin, just as much a part of me as my hands, feet, and weapon. "She fears what may happen if she allows anyone through her defenses, and with good reason, I'd imagine. The scar on her abdomen…" My foot faltered a bit, and Jesh took advantage of my mistake.

His sword cut through the gap in my defenses, hitting me and my shadows with a burst of light. The shadows I'd gathered to block it evaporated on impact, but I threw more and managed to stop him before he actually made contact with my body.

"Good," I nodded my approval of his magic use. "When you're up against Laith, that will do even more damage. My brothers' magic naturally opposes each other, while mine is a relative of both."

Jesh grunted an agreement. "What do you think Diora survived?"

We both paused momentarily, and I ran a hand through my hair. It was sweaty and longer than I liked it, but I wasn't sure

Diora would want Lav's hands in it to cut it, and I wasn't going to do anything that could potentially hurt my mate in any way, including emotionally. "I don't know. She was chained for most of her life, as far as I can tell, and she responds to me as if she thinks I might hurt her if I show any negative emotion even slightly. So probably some kind of torture, too." The admission disturbed me and infuriated me more than I could ever describe.

I forced out a slow breath, pushing away the ferocious power that built up within me. My magic sometimes responded to my emotions when they grew out of control, so I had to be careful with them. "She'll tell me eventually. And when she does, I'll fucking demolish anyone who ever so much as considered hurting her."

"You know I'll be there beside you, brother," Jesh agreed.

I flashed him a grin. "We'll burn the damn world down if we have to."

He chuckled. "If only we had fire magic running through our veins."

Jesh and I returned to our fight, picking up the pace. The dance of our magic and swords growing fiercer and faster. I held back—I always had to hold back, when fighting my friends. Their magic couldn't match mine. Other than my brothers', Diora's was the only person's who could. But she didn't exactly seem keen on learning to fight.

"You need to get her training. You know it won't be long until Laith returns with an army," Jesh warned, as we continued to spar.

I made a noise of disagreement. "She shut the idea down before I could even bring it up. She has no desire to fight, and you know I won't force her."

"She's afraid," Jesh pointed out, bringing my words back to bite me. "The only way she'll defeat that fear is if she learns to control it."

"You and I know that, but she doesn't. And I've barely convinced her not to hate me—I'm not risking her hatred again by trying to force her to do *anything* she doesn't want to do."

"That's your call to make," Jesh agreed. "But the longer you wait, the more you risk her life, and the lives of those in your kingdom."

"Her freedom is worth more to her than her life," I told him, my voice firm. "So that risk is one we're going to have to take."

Jesh nodded, but wore a deep grimace as we both parted for a moment, taking a short break. He grabbed a bottle of water off the side of the room, and I stretched my muscles, trying to get them back into shape after days of wandering the forest with my female.

Jesh called out from the other side of the room, "We're going to need to double the guards and triple the patrols. When Laith finds out that you've found your fated mate, you know he'll do everything in his power to destroy her before you can begin the bond with her. If he can take out Diora, he'll take you out with her."

I dipped my head in a nod. "I set that in motion while you were setting up her tent that first day in the forest. One of his spies is bound to get the information to him sooner rather than later—and I'm not risking her."

He flashed me a smirk, gesturing toward my neck. "She let you into her bed; the bond should begin soon. I'm surprised it's not already written on your flesh."

I chuckled. "Not the way you're thinking. We didn't even cuddle."

Jesh lifted an eyebrow.

"I'm not sure what she even knows about sex or reproduction," I admitted. "I've been trying to find a way to bring it up, but..." I shrugged.

Jesh grimaced "Ask Lav to talk to her."

I shrugged my shoulders. "I don't want her to think I'm trying to push her into my arms like that."

"Aren't you?"

"I want her, but I have no idea what's been done to her—what if she's been raped, or otherwise sexually abused? She either doesn't know anything about sex, or she's had horrible experiences with it to the point where she's not interested in being with me that way, despite us being mates."

"Does she even know anything about your bond?" Jesh suddenly looked skeptical. "What *does* she know? She doesn't exactly seem informed."

I scowled at him. "Talk about her like that and I won't hold my shadows back. You saw the scars on her wrists and ankles; the one on her abdomen is even worse. What she knows doesn't matter; her determination to survive does. And however long it takes, whatever I have to do, I'll prove to her that she can trust me."

"And then you'll fuck her." Jesh grabbed his sword.

"And then I'll *make love* to her." I picked my training sword up off the ground, flipping it in my hands as my shadows slid over the weapon. "Morning and night, for the rest of our fucking lives."

Jesh chuckled. "Did we meet the same woman?"

"I warned you." I let my shadows have their way as I stalked toward my friend. "Speak ill of my mate, and you'll bleed for it."

Chapter 16

Diora

I spent the majority of the day lost in the science and practice of cooking. It was surprisingly easy, with the only problem being that I couldn't read the recipes. By the time the dinner rush came around and the fae chefs kicked me out of their kitchen politely, I'd learned what the words for measurements looked like, and was able to read the recipes with relative ease.

My fingers itched to continue cooking as I slipped out of the dining room, my stomach already full after eating the food I'd cooked, but I didn't have a kitchen. Besides the large one in the dining room, the only one I knew about was Namir's, and no way was I going to ask him to let me borrow his room. He'd assume I was asking him to ignite our bond or something, if that was even possible.

Knowing Namir would come looking for me soon, I had the urge to make a run for it—to slip into the forest for a bit of peace and some time away from the king. He was sweet, and I liked being around him, but our connection was really damn intense.

But he had gone out of his comfort zone with leaving me alone as I cooked that day, so I headed toward the training room instead. Namir's throne was in there still, pressed up against the corner.

There was a crowd inside, so I leaned up against the back wall, watching with reluctant interest as Namir fought four other fae at once. Jesh was barking out orders, advice, and insults to the men fighting the king, but Namir's shadows moved like they were a part of him.

A sleek woman with long, dark red hair leaned up against the wall beside me, catching my attention. Her eyes were lined with makeup, her lashes longer and darker than they'd been the last time I saw her, and the golden dress she wore was clearly made to emphasize both the strength of her muscles and the softness of her curves.

The last time I'd seen her, she'd been wearing white and silver. I couldn't help but wonder if like Namir, she'd dressed the way she did because she didn't want to trigger my darkest memories.

Lavee murmured to me, "Impressive, isn't he?"

A sharp anger had my monster bursting to life. I managed to shove her down, just barely. "Excuse me?"

She glanced over at me. "Jesh, I mean. See how he keeps up with all four of the other fighters, instructing each of them? Namir only honed gifts he was born with; Jesh had to develop his from nothing."

Her words surprised me, but my wolf dissipated completely, which was a damned relief. "Magic is not easily honed. I don't think Namir controls his without a fight."

She nodded. "Touché."

There was a beat of silence as we both watched the fighters dance. "I can do your hair, if you'd like. Jesh suggested I talk to you about sex, anyway."

My eyebrows lifted, and I looked over at her again. "Why would I need you to talk to me about sex?"

She shrugged. "We don't know what you know about it."

I scowled. "Penis goes in vagina. Bodies exude fluids. Supposedly it's pleasurable, somehow."

Lavee snorted. "We need to be friends."

I rolled my eyes. "Because I know about sex?"

"Because you don't take anyone's shit, and I'm all for that."

I supposed that was a decent enough reason.

"There's more to sex than just the physical aspect—and more to the physical aspect than that. Why don't I cut your hair tomorrow morning, and I can explain more while I do?

Considering Namir's a virgin, you'll want all the information I can give you before you take the plunge."

"You're probably right," I admitted. "Will it matter that I'm a virgin, too?"

"Nah. It just means you'll figure that shit out together, and neither of you will realize that it's not good at first." She winked at me, and I rolled my eyes.

The men disbanded, and Namir strode over to me with a massive grin. Beads of sweat dripped off his soaked hair, and his chest gleamed with more evidence of his exertion. He scooped me up off the ground, and I grumbled into his shoulder, "You're all sweaty."

"And now you are too." He was still grinning as he pulled away. "I want you to tell me all about your day while I shower."

"You peeked at me more than two dozen times," I pointed out, as he towed me toward the shadowy doorway off to the side of the stairs.

"Damn straight. I had to make sure Errh wasn't flirting with my female."

My eyes rolled. "And?"

"And he kept a respectable distance. Especially after he noticed me glaring at him."

"I'm sure he appreciated that a lot," I drawled.

Namir laughed, flashing me a playful grin. "Not losing his head for trying to make a move on you? Yes, I'm sure he did appreciate that."

I snorted. "Something tells me your possessiveness is going to become a problem, *Love*."

"You say that like it's not already." His grin morphed into a smirk.

I couldn't help but smirk right back at him, and earned another shit-eating grin in response.

"Stars, you're beautiful when you smile," he remarked, tugging me through the shadowy door and into his room.

HE STARTED THE SHOWER, once again ordering me to tell him about my day of cooking. I was reluctant at first, but bubbling with excitement about the stuff I'd made.

I sat on the floor just inside the door to the bathroom, and he washed quickly as I spoke with more animation than I'd realized I was capable of.

Namir participated in the conversation, asking for more details when I confused him about something. I noticed him grow quiet when I explained memorizing the shape of the words for measurements, so I could figure them out, after someone had told me which order the ingredients were listed in.

When he finally got out of the shower much later than I expected him to (he'd washed really damn slowly), he strolled out of the bathroom with a towel wrapped around his hips.

The towel covered nearly the same amount of skin as his pants usually did, yet something about the way it hugged his backside had that obnoxious heat flaring in my lower belly.

My eyes followed him as he crossed the room, headed toward his closet.

Stars, he was gorgeous.

"You were telling me about cooking desserts," Namir called out to me, as he disappeared into the closet.

Right.

I cleared my throat. "They have to sit for a few hours—I'm going to go back and taste them after the dinner rush."

"Am I invited?"

I rolled my eyes. "I doubt I could prevent you from following me after you left me alone for half the day."

He chuckled. "You know me too well already."

Did I, though?

All I really knew about him was... that he'd waited his whole life to meet his fated mate, and saved himself for her.

For me.

And that he hated mornings. And that he wanted to end the fighting between the different factions of the kingdoms.

And that he had nightmares about his mother's hatred; he had mentioned that to me at one point.

So maybe I knew more about him than I'd realized, but it was far from everything.

"Do you know how to cook?" I asked him, from where I still sat on the floor.

He slipped out of the closet, wearing a pair of black pants and running a hand through his gorgeous wet hair. The motion reminded me that he'd lied to me about *my* hair— which frustrated me once again.

"I don't. My mother would've had at least one or two fae tortured if she knew they had allowed me into the kitchen— probably more. And since she and my father died, my focus has been on surviving a fight with my brothers and their men, as well as protecting my portion of the kingdom."

My head bobbed in a nod, cooking forgotten now that I'd been reminded of his dishonesty. "You lied to me."

He frowned. "No I didn't."

I scowled. "In the forest—you lied about my hair. You said it felt nice, but now I've used your hair soaps, and I know that was a lie."

Understanding dawned in his eyes. "It wasn't."

My scowl deepened, and I stood. My fists clenched at my sides.

Namir crossed the room, capturing my wrist in his hand. "Here, Love. Feel." He lifted my hand to his head, tilting it down so my fingers could slide into his hair. It was wet and a bit cold, but the way my hand brushed his scalp made me shiver a bit. "Your hair didn't feel soft, but the fact that my hands were touching your head, that you trusted me to braid your hair, and that I was doing something for you that you could've done for yourself, made it feel nice."

Oh.

I withdrew my hand from his hair, and he released it. "Do you believe me?"

I nodded in response, stepping back, and his expression relaxed.

"I'm glad you enjoyed cooking. I'd like to teach you to read and write, if that's okay with you—I want you to have those abilities, should you ever need or even just want them."

The words surprised me, but not in an unpleasant way. "I would like that."

His lips curved upward slightly, his smile satisfied. "After dinner every day, we'll practice in here."

I nodded again. "That'll work."

"Good. Will you be cooking again tomorrow?"

The fact that he asked, and that he left it as an option, made me feel better about our strange relationship. "I'd like to learn something else tomorrow. The chefs said there are people who create ceramic dishes in the city—I'm going to find them, and ask them to teach me. Considering my relationship with you, I doubt they'll turn me down."

He flashed me a grin. "Finally, you've realized the benefits of being fated to a well-loved king."

I snorted. "Hardly. I just want to try things, now that I'm not locked up anymore."

His grin vanished at the mention of my past. "I'll ask someone to take a note to the ceramicists after dinner, to get it set up."

I nodded. Lavee was going to do my hair in the morning, but I didn't think the haircut and sex conversation would take that long. I did know the basics, and since Lavee did hair professionally, I couldn't imagine she was slow when it came to a simple haircut. Akari had told me of the wild things some fae did with their hair—changing its color, adding more colors, lightening some strands... it was hard for me to imagine.

"Let me grab food, and then we'll start our first lesson.

I flashed him a small smile. "I'll wait here; I ate after I cooked."

He squeezed my hand—I hadn't noticed him take it, surprisingly enough—and then slipped out of the room, through the shadows.

They closed behind him, leaving me staring after him for a moment before I finally turned to survey his space. It was the first time I'd been in there alone. Curiosity nudged me to go through all of his things, to see what he valued enough to keep in his personal space.

But I ignored that curiosity, instead making my way into his kitchen. Opening the fridge, I looked for food, and found only something thin, brown, and rectangular, wrapped in thin, dark brown paper. I pulled it out, unwrapping the side to peer at the food.

It was smooth, and hard.

Hmm.

It almost resembled the chocolate we had used to cook in the kitchen that day, and that shit had been delicious.

I lifted the package to my nose, and sniffed it. There was a slightly sweet smell, but it wasn't strong.

Using my fingers, I snapped off a small piece at the end, and lifted it to my lips. My eyes closed as the thick, sweet taste coated my tongue.

Fuck.

It was the same as the chocolate in the kitchen, but better. So damn much better.

I opened the fridge again, looking for more of the chocolate, but didn't find any. I wanted to devour the rest of the candy I'd found, but didn't want to anger Namir by doing so without asking.

So, with heavy eyes focused on the chocolate, I rewrapped it and stuck it back in the fridge.

My feet were slow and my mood wistful as I made my way over to the couch to wait for Namir to return.

Chapter 17

He didn't keep me waiting long, coming back in with two plates of steaming food in his hands, despite my warning that I wasn't hungry.

Namir set the plates down on the table between the two couches, and grabbed a large book off one of his bookshelves. He walked around for a moment, finding a sheet of paper and a writing utensil that he called a pen.

After he placed the paper on top of the book, he wrote on it for a moment, and then placed it down on the table just in front of me. He explained that those were letters, and taught me the names of each of them as he ate, followed by the sounds each of them made.

I learned quickly, but it was a lot to remember.

When we took our first break from learning, giving my brain a bit of a rest, I brought up the chocolate. His eyes lit up when I did, and he got it out, rewarding me with squares of the candy as chunks of time passed. It was so damned delicious that I didn't even mind the fact that he was bribing me.

When my head felt like it might explode a few hours later, I finally declared the lesson over, much to Namir's amusement. We slipped out of his room together, and headed to the kitchen to taste the desserts I'd created.

The kitchen was empty when we walked through the doors, and it felt a bit eerie to be in there alone.

Namir's hand wrapped around my bicep loosely, his touch comforting me, surprisingly enough. He flipped the lights on, and my gaze followed them across the ceiling as they lit up.

They were incredible—not that the king thought there was anything remarkable about the lighting he'd undoubtedly grown up seeing.

"What did you make?" Namir asked, leaning up against an empty table as I slipped into the kitchen, heading toward the fridge and freezer in the back where we'd put my desserts.

"A chocolate cake, and something called ice cream," I explained, as I tugged the door open.

"Damn, woman. You're going to spoil me," Namir teased.

I rolled my eyes. "I'm sure."

He chuckled as I carried the chocolate cake out first, leaving the ice cream for afterward. He sat down while I set it in front of him, then headed back into the kitchen to grab plates, forks, and a knife to cut the beast.

It had two different kinds of chocolate frosting on it, one thicker and one creamier. I couldn't remember the names for them, but I had tasted each of them, and they were delicious separately. I hoped they were even better together, too.

Namir put a hand on mine before I lifted the knife to the cake. "Why don't we just... eat it?" He grabbed a fork, his eyes gleaming as he lifted it toward the dessert.

"I'm trying to learn how to be civil and have manners," I complained, waving my own fork toward his.

He flashed me a grin. "Manners and civility are overrated, Love. Live a little."

I scowled...

But then I lifted my fork directly to my cake, and cut into it.

The king's laugh about made me grin, but my eyes closed in bliss as the overwhelming chocolate taste soaked my tongue. A groan escaped me. "Maybe I should cook again tomorrow."

He laughed again, louder, and I heard him cut into the cake with his own fork.

"Well?" I asked him, opening my eyes and narrowing them at him when I didn't hear him moan with appreciation the way I had.

"It's delicious," he offered, taking his fork back to the cake for another bite.

I scowled, batting his fork away with mine. "You like chocolate, otherwise you wouldn't have had it in your fridge."

He grinned. "I do. It's just not the taste I've been dreaming about lately."

My eyes narrowed further. "What's that supposed to mean?"

He abandoned his fork, reaching for my face with one hand. His thumb dragged over my lip slowly, dipping into my mouth for a moment before he finally dragged his hand back to his lips. My narrowed eyes turned to daggers as he slipped his thumb into his own mouth, closing his eyes. His chest rumbled slightly as a low groan escaped him.

Fuck.

My lower half was heated again, my body flaring with lust once more.

Damn him.

His eyes opened, his gaze dark. "You've told me little about your past, Diora, but from what I've gathered, you experienced much pain. I can offer you pleasure that won't erase those memories—but will balance them out instead."

My throat swelled, my lower bits throbbing.

I stabbed my fork back into my cake. "Keep talking like that and I'm going to withdraw your standing invitation to sleep in my room, *Love*."

He barked out a laugh. "Stars, you're lovely."

My eyes rolled. "Shut up and enjoy the cake, bastard."

He did as I commanded—though he was grinning the entire time.

WE COULDN'T FINISH the cake, or the ice cream, so we snuck them into Namir's kitchen and left them in his fridge and freezer before heading up to my room.

His hair had only just barely dried after his shower, but I felt dirty after playing with so many food ingredients, so I slipped into the bathroom to wash up. My body was tired, but pleasantly so—and my mind was worn out too, but in a way I loved.

I put my hair up so it wouldn't get wet—it wasn't dirty, and still felt incredibly soft—before slipping into the shower and turning the water on. My eyes closed and my mind wandered as the relaxing heat fell from above.

It felt good to have learned, and had new experiences that day. Never in my life had I done so many new things before, and I absolutely loved knowing that I had. I was learning to read—and eventually write. And I had learned to cook. I was nowhere near professional at it, but after I learned to read, I would be able to stumble my way through a recipe with relative ease.

Learning so many new things was a rush, but my mind kept returning to the words Namir had said to me at the table.

"I can offer you pleasure."

Maybe it had been the taste of the chocolate cake lingering in my mouth at the time, or the thrill of learning new skills, or the way my mind kept going back to his hand on my thigh that morning, but his offer was tempting.

Very, very tempting.

He hadn't asked me to fuck him, or stripped in front of me so I had no choice but to see his naked body—he'd asked to give me pleasure.

And damn, that was tempting.

I'd spent my entire life either in a cell with two other women or in a room being tortured—there had been no pleasure for me. I knew that theoretically, I could figure out how to give that to myself, but...

Well, Namir was my fated mate. And he was absolutely gorgeous. And he had *offered* to give me pleasure.

"Am I really considering this?" I whispered to myself. The noise of the falling water from the shower heads would prevent Namir from hearing me, I knew.

I didn't have to answer the question out loud; I already knew the truth.

I was definitely, definitely considering it.

There were so many things I had never had the chance to try, or do. So many things I had missed out on. And the pleasure of sex was one of them.

My mind went back to the way he'd dragged his thumb over my lip—the way he'd taken it into his own mouth afterward, and groaned at the taste of me and chocolate on his tongue.

My body flushed.

He had offered me pleasure, and...

I wanted it.

My hands were shaking a bit as I turned the water off.

My stomach clenched pleasantly, my lower half hot and achy as I reached out for the towel and found the robe.

Rather than just drying off with it and ditching it in the bathroom, I left it on and padded out into the bedroom.

I found Namir sitting on the bed, staring up at the ceiling, until I stepped out. His gaze immediately fell to me, and then his expression grew hot.

Remaining silent, I walked to the edge of the bed and sat down, tucking a leg up onto the mattress to keep my balance. His gaze dipped to the bare flesh I exposed, and his eyes grew darker and more intense.

"You said you could offer me pleasure," I told him, fighting the urge to wrap my arms around myself.

I was strong; I was a survivor. I could talk about sex and pleasure without feeling the need to cover myself further, or hide.

"I did."

"Does the offer stand?" I asked, slipping my hands beneath my thighs so they wouldn't reveal my anxiety.

"Always."

I let out a slow, quiet breath, then stood and slipped the robe off my shoulders. The fabric hit the floor, and the king sat up, sliding to the edge of the bed. His feet touched the ground, and I remained where I was, his head level with my breasts.

"I'll need to touch you, first. To figure out what feels good for you," he murmured, his hands remaining by his sides.

"I don't know how you'd pleasure me without your hands," I drawled back. "Do you even know what you're doing?"

He barked out a laugh. "Theoretically."

I snorted. "Maybe I should find someone else to teach me pleasure."

His humor vanished, and he stood abruptly, his eyes burning into mine. "Not a fucking chance." He stepped around me, and I held my chin high as I felt his eyes on my skin while he slowly circled me, his gaze taking in every detail of my body. "You're the most beautiful thing I've ever seen, Diora—you're fucking breathtaking. My salvation—my fate—my mate."

I flushed further with his words.

His fingers finally made contact with me, dragging lightly over my rib cage as he stepped around the front of me. His attention was focused on my body, now, and my eyes closed as his touch dipped to the scar on my abdomen. "Does it hurt here?"

"No," I mumbled.

"Is it sensitive, though?"

"Not physically."

Mentally, it was another story.

To feel fingers on my skin, on the place even I hadn't been able to touch for twenty years...

Stars.

"What about here?" His second hand brushed one of my wrists.

"No," I whispered again.

"Open your eyes, Love. I want you to look at me while I touch you."

His words made me shudder, but I forced my eyes to open. They locked with his, and my abdomen clenched when I saw that small, sexy smirk on his face while he touched me.

"Stars, you're proud of yourself," I mumbled to him.

He chuckled. "Not proud of myself, Diora; proud of you. My gorgeous wolf, letting me take care of her."

I scowled. "I'm not a wolf."

"Agree to disagree." His fingers continued moving over my scar as he walked another slow circle around my body, and I had to clench my jaw to keep my eyes open. "How does this feel?" His palms met my bare sides, and I inhaled sharply. "Diora?"

"Good," I managed.

His palms slid over my scar, up my ribcage, and wrapped around my breasts. "And this?"

My breaths were shallow, my body tight. "Good."

His palms massaged my breasts slowly, for a moment, and picked up the pace as his thumbs brushed my nipples. My hips jerked slightly, my ass meeting his thighs as I stumbled backward.

He held me to his chest, his fingers still playing with my nipples. "And this?"

"So good," I moaned softly.

His erection throbbed against my lower back, and my breathing grew even more rapid at the feel of his desire against me.

"Does it feel good for you?" I asked, panting a bit.

"We're not worrying about me right now," he murmured.

"Namir," I growled back.

"Yes, Love, it feels incredible." His voice was lower than it had been a moment earlier, and more gravelly too. "You feel like fucking heaven in my hands."

The words had me rocking back a bit more, my ass still on his thighs and his erection still throbbing against my lower back.

He pinched my nipples softly, and I cried out.

His shadows wrapped around us, holding us in a bubble away from the outside world. One of his hands slid off my breast, down my body, and stroked the sensitive skin between my thighs. I cried out again as his fingers slid between my folds, and he growled against my shoulder, his lips latching on to my skin and sucking lightly.

His fingers found my clit—my most sensitive part—and I rocked against him harder, my cries growing louder and more desperate as he touched me, stroked me, played with me. "And how does that feel?"

I couldn't gather my thoughts enough to speak, so his fingers paused on my core and breast.

His erection throbbed against my lower back.

"How is it, Diora?" His teeth scraped my shoulder.

Need and fury hit me so hard that I snarled, "It's fucking incredible, Namir. Keep going, or I'll—"

A sharp cry tore through me as he resumed his touch.

The pressure that had built inside me shattered, and I went over the edge with a sound that was nearly a scream. Pleasure rolled through my body, tearing my control and need and everything else away. There was just me, Namir, his fingers, and his erection throbbing against my spine.

We dropped to the bed together, both of us panting. His hand was still buried between my thighs, his erection damp against my lower back. He must've found his pleasure when I did—without requiring so much as a single touch from my fingers.

Pride swelled in me at that thought—Akari had told me how needy most men were, but Namir hadn't asked me for a damned thing.

"How did that feel?" I whispered to Namir, my body still wrapped around his hand.

"Better than anything I've ever imagined," he growled softly into my neck, into my hair. "You've ruined me, Love."

I snorted. "What does that mean?"

"It means now that I've felt you lose it in my arms, heard the sexy little noises you make when you come, you'll never be rid of me." His teeth scraped my neck, and I jerked a bit, wiggling against him as a laugh burst out of me.

His lips curved upward against my throat. "A smile and a laugh in the same day? Stars, I'm a lucky man."

I rolled my eyes and swatted at his arm. "You're insufferable."

"Yet you love to suffer me," he purred.

I snorted again. He wasn't wrong—and I loved that he wasn't.

His arms tightened around me. "Tell me you'll sleep naked in my arms tonight."

"I did last night. You rolled off your side of the bed and into mine," I grumbled.

His eyebrows lifted. "I did?"

"Yes. I had to use my shadows to get out from underneath your heavy ass."

He tickled my side, and I shrieked, bucking against him. My head crashed into his chin, and we both groaned.

"Damn you," I grumbled, reaching up to rub the budding bruise on my skull.

"I'm proud of you, Love. It takes a lot of focus to manipulate the shadows that well," he said, his voice light but honest.

"Thanks, I guess." I shrugged a bit awkwardly. "What do we do now?"

"Now I clean my release off your back, take a quick shower, and then collapse into bed with you," he teased lightly.

I shut my eyes. "Alright. If you're too slow, I'll fall asleep without you."

He chuckled, pressing his lips to my shoulder. "Understood."

CHAPTER 18

I WOKE up in the middle of the night, after a steamy dream that featured Namir's hands on all my most sensitive bits. Panting, I looked around for the king, and found him sprawled halfway over my body again. His erection wasn't between my thighs that time, but I wanted to see it—and feel it.

And stars, I wanted him to touch me again.

I poked and prodded at his arms and shoulder, trying to wake him up, but got only grumpy grunts and mumbled complaints for my effort. Deciding to take things in my hands—literally—I shoved my hand between our pelvises and reached into his pants.

My fingers wrapped around his thick, silky warmth, and my eyebrows shot upward.

Damn, he was huge.

Was that normal?

Would that thing really fit inside me?

He groaned when I squeezed him, sliding my hand over him.

His eyes opened, and he peered down at me, sleepy and shocked and hot as hell. "What are you doing, Love?" His voice was a sexy growl that only made me hot again.

"Touching you. Is that alright?" I asked, already knowing the answer.

"Any fucking time you want. Always. Forever."

"I don't know what I'm doing," I warned. "But it woke your grumpy ass up, so..."

He rolled me over, pinning me beneath him. Maybe it should've scared me, but all it did was ignite me. I wanted him—needed him.

"Woke my grumpy ass up, huh?" His eyes gleamed with mischief as he tugged my hand away from his erection, rocking against me and hitting all of the right places as he did so. He still had his silky pants on, but they only made the friction smoother, and hotter.

"Mmhm," I replied breathlessly.

"Why did you want me awake?" His gaze was wicked.

"I dreamed about you, touching me."

His gaze darkened. "You had a wet dream? Fuck, Love. I thought you never dreamed."

"I don't—I didn't. This was only my second dream, ever," I admitted.

"And it was about me? That's fucking incredible." He rolled us back over, but sat up with his legs out in front of him and me sitting on his lap, straddling him. His erection met my core, and he was hard as a damn rock. "I'm going to kiss you now, Diora."

"Oh, am I *Diora* when you're preparing to kiss me, instead of your *Love*?" I practically purred the words, emphasizing his accent and making him grin.

"Don't distract me when I'm thinking about your lips, *Diora, Love*," he drawled both names back, making me laugh. "Fuck, I love your laugh."

He didn't bother to press his lips to mine lightly, or hesitate in the slightest; he just captured my face in his hands, and kissed the hell out of me.

Namir's tongue slid into my mouth, his lips soft and warm on mine as they grew acquainted. Neither of us moved to escalate the kiss, focused on the sensations and the way our bodies were pressed together. The only thing that separated us was those damned pants, but I was in no hurry to undress the king—not when he kissed me like he was.

Time passed as our tongues danced, our shadows intertwining around us while we continued tasting each other. Eventually, our hands began to move—to touch, to explore one another. His were on my back, my arms, my breasts. Mine were on his biceps, his shoulders, his abdomen. He was a work of art, and the way he touched me was almost as perfect as the man himself.

Our touches grew hotter, and needier, until Namir landed on his back on the bed, with me still positioned over him. Our mouths continued to move together as I began rocking against his erection, rubbing him against me, and moaning into his mouth when the tension within me grew tighter and more demanding.

The pressure within me finally came unraveled, and I groaned into his mouth as he rocked against me, harder and faster. His teeth bit down on my lip just hard enough to draw a little blood as he snarled into my mouth, and I cried out as another orgasm tore through me with the pleasurable pain.

It was such a small cut—and one caused by nothing but passion.

And I fucking loved it.

"Shit, Diora." Namir pulled his lips from mine, panting. His eyes were wild and his hair was messy, but his hands were on my face, his thumb moving my lip around carefully as he checked out the injury he'd given me. "Fuck, Love. I'm so sorry."

"I liked it," I admitted.

He scoffed. "Don't lie to me."

I scowled back. "I'm not lying. It felt good."

His scoff turned into a furious expression that surprised me. "I fucking hurt you, Diora. Don't try to tell me that's okay." He rolled me back to my side of the bed, his arms unwrapping from around me. My core was damp with his release and my own body's reaction to him, and I loved that too.

But he seemed determined to hate it, so I glared back at him as he sat up and shoved his hands into his hair.

"Be as angry as you want," I growled back at him. "But don't just go and assume you understand my feelings." I rolled to my side.

Namir's hand landed on my thigh. His voice wasn't playful, or soft, for once. "Diora, Love..."

"Don't '*Diora, Love*' me," I snarled back. "If you'd really hurt me, I would've told you."

"I'm sorry."

Great.

Now he was apologizing for fucking me with our clothes on.

"Goodnight," I growled back at him.

He shoved his hand through his hair again. "I'm going to take a shower."

I didn't respond; what was I going to say? I'm sorry you're sorry that I loved what we did and you didn't?

Stars, this was a shitty situation.

He slipped off the bed, heading into the bathroom. The shower turned on yet again, and I closed my eyes as the Shadow King washed himself clean. Eventually, I managed to push away the memory of his apology, and fell back asleep.

LAVEE ERASED the awkwardness of the next morning by banging on my door before either of us was awake. Namir snarled curses at the door, while I stumbled out of bed and padded across the room.

I tugged the door open, and Lavee's eyebrows shot upward as she looked at me. "Do you always answer the door like this?"

I glanced down at myself.

Naked again.

Shit.

Slamming the door shut in her face, I ignored Namir's cursing as he rolled out of bed and followed me into the closet.

"We need to talk," he warned me.

"You need to stop getting mad every time I accidentally flash someone," I growled back.

He flung his hands into the air. "What am I going to do with you, woman?"

"You could start with apologizing for last night." I tossed a hand toward the bed. "I had a perfectly nice time, and you ruined it."

He scoffed. "I know I ruined it, Diora. Why do you think I was so pissed?"

"No, you ruined it by getting frustrated with yourself, not by biting me. I fucking loved it when you bit me." I spun to face the clothes, and grabbed the first dress and undergarment I saw, tugging them off their hangers.

His hand was gentle as he set it on my arm. "How could you love that after what you survived?"

I shoved his hand off me, snarling, "You have *no idea* what I survived, Namir. You don't get to assume you know what I'll like, dislike, or hate just because of whatever you think I've lived through."

"Then tell me." His hands spread wide, his shadows dancing off his skin almost... angrily. They were reacting to his emotions, and if I hadn't been so frustrated, I would've been enthralled by them.

"No." My voice went flat.

I yanked my underclothing up my body, reaching around to find the zipper. Namir stepped behind me and zipped it up for me without asking or waiting for me to ask.

He let out a slow breath. "Alright, Love. I'm sorry for pushing. I shouldn't have let my emotions get the best of me." He released the zipper and stepped away "Lavee can't expect me to train this early. Is she here for you?"

"She's cutting my hair," I said stiffly.

The sex conversation would not be mentioned. Not even maybe.

"That's nice of her." He gave me a small, playful smile, but I was starting to see through the show he put on for his kingdom. He wasn't always happy, like he wanted people to believe—and he wasn't always laughing.

"It is." My emotions were too much of a mess for me to bring up his façade, so I didn't.

"I trust you'll be safe with her." One of his hands slipped into his pants' pocket. "Don't leave the castle without me, please?"

"Mmhm." My voice came out clipped.

"Thank you." He caught my hand and lifted it to his lips, pressing a kiss to the back of my palm. "I'm sorry for whatever you want me to be sorry for, Love. I just want you safe, and secure, and happy." His words were genuine, but I was still frustrated.

And still unsure how much of his behavior was just his princely mask, and how much was his genuine attitude.

When I nodded, he released my hand, and then slipped out of the closet while I tugged my dress over my shoulders.

Namir murmured a greeting to Lavee as he opened the door, him stepping out of the room while she strode into it.

She lifted an eyebrow toward me as I came out of my closet, tugging my hair out from within my dress. "That didn't seem like the Namir I know."

"I know," I grumbled, gesturing her toward the bathroom.

Namir had a few different pairs of dirty pants in the hamper, so I tossed a damp towel over the top of them to hide them. He must've brought the spare towels in himself, or known where they were stored; I'd only ever noticed the robe before.

"I know him better than most. I might be able to give you advice," she remarked, unzipping a palm-sized, round case as she gestured for me to stand in front of her.

"Noted," I drawled.

She grinned, but didn't call me on it again. "So you just want to trim the ends?" She picked up strands of my tangled hair, inspecting the ends. "Or do you want something entirely different?"

I studied my reflection in the mirror.

I'd had long hair my entire life; it would feel strange to remove it. Maybe a good type of strange, though.

But was I ready for yet another change? My life had been full of them lately.

"I'll think about cutting it off," I finally said. "But right now, I don't know if I'm ready. Let's just trim the ends."

She nodded. "Of course."

Lavee dragged her comb quickly through my hair, tugging out knots. She seemed to be watching to see if I felt any pain as she did so, but I was far too used to being yanked around by my hair to flinch at a bit of combing.

"Do you still want me to tell you about sex?" Her eyes remained on my hair as she spoke.

I sighed. "No. I think we're figuring it out."

Her eyebrows shot upward. "Then why the hell was Namir so bothered?"

I debated keeping it quiet, but figured she really might have useful ideas. "Have you had sex before?"

She snorted. "Plenty. It's been a long while, but it's not something a person forgets."

"Namir and I didn't go all the way, I suppose. Just touching and whatnot. But when we were kissing, he bit my lip, and assumed I'd hated it and was angry with him. Even after I told him I'd liked it, he was still upset. He didn't believe me."

I shrugged. "So we're in a fight, sort of. But he's still trying to act like his playful self."

Lavee's expression grew thoughtful. "Do you want my true feelings, or should I soften them?"

"I am not a soft person, Lavee," I grumbled back.

She grinned. "You can call me Lav. Most of my friends do. And... I think Namir probably scared himself."

I blinked. "He what?"

"He's the youngest of the three brothers, and he never makes offensive moves against Laith and Espen. Honestly, I think he's hoping one of them will call for a peace treaty of some sort, so he doesn't have to hurt either of them. Maybe with you, he lost himself to his passion for the first time in his life, and it scared him. Of course, that's just me thinking aloud." She pulled a pair of small shears from the case she'd brought. "Stare straight forward and try not to move."

I followed her instructions. "You know him far better than I do."

Lavee made a noncommittal sound. "I'm not sure anyone really knows Namir. He doesn't speak of his past, and as I'm sure you've realized, he refuses to acknowledge any potentially pessimistic future. When Jesh or I try to get him to open up, he shuts down. You're probably the only person he'll truly let in, given how long he's been waiting to find you."

Her words surprised me... but not in a bad way.

"What would you do, if you were me?" I asked, curiously.

She laughed. "I would already have fucked him."

I couldn't help but laugh with her. "He's gorgeous," I admitted.

"If you like the muscled, grinning, pretty-boy type," she teased.

"And what do you prefer?" I countered.

Her gaze grew a bit forlorn. "The massive, rough type unfortunately."

"Are you talking about Jesh?"

"Mmhm." She focused on my hair for a bit. "He and I are the talk of the town; fated mates who choose not to embrace our connection. If you haven't heard the gossip about us yet, you will soon."

My eyebrows shot upward. "You don't want to be fated?"

"Not according to the gossipers."

My eyes narrowed at her in the mirror. "I'm asking *you*."

She sighed. "It's complicated."

I waited.

The only sound for a moment was that of her scissors snipping bits of my hair, but then she finally spoke again.

"Jesh has a poor opinion of fated pairings. He doesn't want children, either, and I'm sure you know that mated pairs are the only ones who can produce them. There's no birth control that can prevent pregnancy in a mated pair, either, so it's not as if we could be one thing but not the other."

Shit.

I hadn't known that, actually.

That meant Namir's parents had been fated... and mine had been too. I knew mine had been lost during childbirth—fated mates lived and died as one. But I regretted never having the chance to meet them. I'd daydreamed about them as a child, imagining a life where I would get to play in the forests I could only attempt to imagine, loved by people I could only wish I'd known.

And they had been a mated pair...

Stars, I hoped they'd loved each other fiercely while they had the chance.

That knowledge brought a level of uncertainty to the possibility of having sex with Namir, though. If there was no way to prevent pregnancy, I might be getting myself into a hell of a lot more than a good time if we went all the way.

"And what about you?" I asked Lavee.

She gave me a small smile. "I'm still trying to wrap my head around the fact that I'll spend my immortal life alone. Jesh is happy to be my friend, but..." she trailed off, shrugging a bit.

"But you don't want to be just friends."

"Unfortunately not. So, I try to spend plenty of time out and away from the castle, in hopes that by some miracle, I'll find a man who's interested in a serious relationship with someone he's not fated to."

"Wow, Lav. That's terrible. If it makes you feel any better, I spent the first twenty-one years of my life being tortured."

We both stared at each other in the mirror for a long moment, before we burst out laughing.

"Aren't we just a sad pair of fuckers," she said with a grin, wiping at the corners of her eyes with the side of her hands.

"Mmhm. Don't tell Namir about that last bit—he's not going to find out until I feel like I can trust him."

"You don't think you can trust him yet?" Her words were curious.

I shrugged. "I do, mostly. But like you said, he has a lot more secrets than he's admitted to any of us. I'm not going to spill my soul to him before I've seen at least some of his."

Lavee nodded, and resumed trimming my hair. "I always wondered what his fated mate would be like. I imagined her much more... smiley. I'm glad she's not."

"Strangely enough, I think I am too," I admitted.

The topic changed to hair products, and she checked what I had in my shower before tossing it in the trash bin and promising to retrieve some better hair shit for me from her room before I washed up. The conversation didn't grow serious again, but I enjoyed it. And by the time she left me to wash my newly-trimmed hair, I felt like I might've made my first real friend outside of the prison I'd spent so much of my life in.

Not counting Namir, of course; things between him and I were too complex to define yet.

CHAPTER 19

I FOUND Namir waiting on the couches downstairs, chatting with a fae woman I didn't recognize when I finally went out to find him. My monster gathered in my abdomen immediately, but I forced myself to notice how much space there was between Namir and the beautiful woman—and how practiced the smile on his face was.

He wasn't happy to be talking to her. Not really. He wanted people to believe he was, but that had to be just part of his kingly mask.

My monster dissipated, especially when Namir's eyes left the woman and landed on me, then trailed down my body appreciatively. He didn't seem to notice my haircut, but I didn't give a damn about that.

"If you'll excuse me, my queen's ready for me," he told the other woman, standing and striding toward me without a glance back toward her.

I lifted an eyebrow at him as he took my arm and swept me toward the doors that led out of the castle. "We don't have any markings on our throats to suggest that our bond has developed," I reminded him.

"Semantics," he said, his voice smooth and upbeat.

How much of that cheerfulness was a front?

Was he only putting on a grin for everyone else's sake?

"Where are we going?" I changed the subject. Out in public in his kingdom clearly wasn't a place for me to call him on his shit, if there was a place at all.

"The ceramicists. I'll be running my training out in the streets, to keep my warriors on their toes."

He'd remembered.

Despite everything else, I grudgingly admitted to myself that the gesture was sweet.

"To make it possible to check on me half a dozen times every hour, you mean," I drawled back.

He flashed me a playful smile. "You know me too well, Love."

"Do I?" I shot back.

His eyes narrowed a bit, though his smile remained. "What did you and Lavee talk about this morning?"

"Sex," I lied smoothly.

His eyes went back to their normal shape, his gaze returning to the horizon as we continued to walk. "And?"

"And I didn't know that there's no form of birth control that works on fated mates," I admitted.

That one wasn't a lie at all.

Namir nodded. "I would've made sure you knew, had I thought we were at that point in our relationship yet."

Honestly, I believed him. The way he'd reacted when he bit my lip definitely didn't make me think he'd be alright with secretly impregnating me.

"Then you agree that we can't have full-out sex yet. We need to make sure we're thinking clearly and on the same page before we risk bringing a child into the world; we can't go there unless we're ready to be parents."

"I agree." Namir's voice was still upbeat, though the topic of our conversation didn't really feel like an upbeat one.

Feeling a bit self-conscious, I added, "There's a lot we still don't know about each other—particularly about our pasts. We should know each other extremely well before we contemplate having a child together; I don't even know whether or not your kingdom is safe for kids."

Namir whirled to face me, his hands cradling my cheeks and his gaze deathly serious. "We can put off the sex and anything else as long as we need to, Diora, but never doubt whether or not you're safe. I will always protect you and any child we bring into this world; always."

The fervent promises in his voice were intense enough to take my breath away a bit.

"Alright," I said, not sure what else there was to say.

He released my face a few moments later, stepping back a bit to give me space, and then gestured toward a building we'd stopped in front of. "Here we are, Love." His grin was back, but it was the practiced, kingly one.

Not ready to call him out for that fake grin yet, I slipped into the ceramicists' studio, and spent the day lost in their work.

THE NEXT FEW weeks passed by quickly, and similarly.

I spent a day or two learning the beginning of a new craft or trade, rotating through everything Namir or I could come up with in an attempt to discover what I liked most. Though I enjoyed almost all of them, none of them stuck out as something I'd want to do every day for the rest of my life, except maybe cooking. And the chefs had pretty much told me that wasn't going to happen given the fact that I was Namir's fated mate.

Me and Namir continued to spend our evenings in his space, while he taught me to read and write. We stayed longer and longer each night, distracting ourselves from discussing topics that neither of us seemed willing to bring up.

Despite our avoidance of any conversation resembling sex and all other truly serious topics, we had fun together. He cracked jokes, I replied with sarcasm, and we could usually volley back and forth until we were both grinning.

But he didn't open up about his past to me, and I didn't open up about mine to him.

Still, every night we played around in my bed together, both of us naked as we learned to bring each other pleasure without letting our bodies truly connect.

Lavee convinced me to spend one or two days a week in her hair salon, with her and her many friends there. The fae there were chatty and gossiped like mad, but it was fun to be around them anyway. Lav had taught me how to blow hair dry with a device made for that purpose, and though I didn't really enjoy doing it, I had to admit I was getting quite good at it.

But by the time my fifth week in the castle rolled around, I was starting to get frustrated with my situation.

Not my living situation; I loved the castle, and the city, and even the kingdom. Hell, I loved my life, there.

But I was frustrated with Namir's practiced grins and the way he avoided discussing his past.

So, near the end of the fifth week, when we closed our lettering books, I didn't get up with Namir. Instead, I remained seated on the couch, with my legs tucked up under my ass.

"What are you doing?" His voice was as playful as always, his hands braced on the back of his couch as he leaned a bit closer to me. There was intrigue in his eyes, and as far as I could tell, his emotions were genuine for the moment.

"I think I'll stay in here tonight," I remarked, turning and laying on my side on the couch, so my legs were draped over the cushions too.

"Will you?" Namir flashed me one of his playful smiles. It was one of the genuine ones, and I fucking loved those.

"Yep. You did offer it to me when I was choosing a room."

"I did." He leaned a bit further over the back of the couch. "Why the sudden change of heart?"

"You've proven yourself trustworthy for the most part, and we spend every night together anyway. Might as well sleep under the stars." I gestured toward the massive mattress that hadn't been touched since Namir and I met.

"Well, I'm certainly not opposed to the idea," he stood up straight, slipping his hands into his pockets. "Are you ready for bed now?"

"Mmhm," I agreed, though I made no move to get up.

His eyes only lit up further with interest. "What game are you playing here, Love?"

It wasn't a game—and I felt a bit bad for making him think it might be one.

"Do you remember the first time you kissed me?" I asked him. We'd spent hours and hours with our lips locked since then, our hands exploring each other's bodies while our mouths made love.

"Of course I do." His voice grew lower and sexier.

"Do you remember when you bit me?" He had been careful not to do so again—so, so careful.

The humor and interest in his eyes vanished completely, his body stiffening. "I think about that every single day."

Something told me he didn't think *positively* about it every single day.

But we were making progress, I thought. This one awkward conversation could lead to another, more awkward, more important one. And we needed that.

"So why haven't you done it again?"

His expression darkened further. "I hurt you, Diora. I'm the fucker who's supposed to protect you, and I hurt you."

Now that we were getting into the meat of the conversation, I dropped the pretenses. My feet hit the floor as I stood too.

"You've been holding yourself back since then; I can tell. And I'm tired of this distance between us, okay? I want to see you passionate, and I want to see you lose control with me. I don't want you to be afraid of hurting me; I didn't survive hell to be treated like a damned ceramic doll."

His expression darkened. "You want to see me passionate?"

"Hell yes, I do."

He crossed the room so fast I barely had time to blink.

My back hit the bookshelves—hard.

Namir's tongue was in my mouth instantly, and it felt like he was devouring me whole. His hands were hot on my hips, his mouth brutal against mine, his teeth scraping my lip every time he had the chance.

Our hands moved over each other desperately, until mine were in his pants and his were between my thighs. And then he was touching me, rubbing me, working me.

I shattered a moment later, crying out into his mouth with the fierce pleasure as I stroked him hard and fast. His erection throbbed in my fist as I came, and his release soaked both my hand and his pants.

His forehead crashed into mine, his eyes closed and his expression one of tortured bliss.

"If you're worrying about hurting me right now, I'll claw your balls out myself," I growled at him.

A laugh burst from him—a real laugh, not one of the light, fake ones he gave most of his people. "Stars, you're lovely."

"That's not usually how a person responds to a threat, Namir," I grumbled, though my lips were curved upward in a slight smile as I spoke.

He chuckled, burying his hand into my hair and tilting my head up slightly, so our noses met.

My eyes remained closed, my damp palm still in his pants as I said, "We need to talk about our pasts."

He sighed. "And our future."

As much as I didn't want to talk about what had happened before, I knew that we needed to. Especially if we were going to make decisions about what was coming next for us.

CHAPTER 20

WE WASHED UP TOGETHER, and then returned to the couch. This time, we sat on the same one. Our backs rested against the arm rests and our legs sprawled out over each other's bodies, tangling and bending awkwardly, but giving us a way to see each other's eyes.

"Why do you feel so strongly that you need to protect me?" I asked, starting the conversation. "I know the bond is part of it, but we don't have any markings on our throats yet, so it shouldn't be *that* strong."

He grimaced, but didn't answer immediately.

I figured I'd better soften him up by sharing information about myself first.

"I don't know the names of the people who held my friends and I captive," I admitted. "Their magic was from our land, though. Vena and Akari are both from other lands, so I assume they knew what they were talking about when they told me it was night magic."

Namir's expression darkened as I spoke. His playfulness had vanished, and I was glad it had. I wanted him to be raw and honest with me, not to put on a mask and play the part he thought he needed to. "I hate that you were in pain and I couldn't help you."

I countered, "I hate that you think you hurt me and didn't believe me when I said you didn't."

He shoved a hand through his hair, mussing the dark strands. "My father and mother were fated. He loved her, and any fool could see that she loved him too. But my brother Laith was the only one she ever loved other than him—to everyone else, she was cruel, and hateful."

He continued, his eyes focused on something past me. "My oldest brother, Espen, was always quiet and gentle. He didn't stand up for himself against her; I had to do that for him. She beat us, and though I was close with my father, he didn't stop her. He loved her too much to do so, and didn't love us enough I suppose. Since her passing, I've been paranoid about becoming my mother, about hurting those I'm supposed to love. And about becoming my father, too lost in love to defend those I need to protect."

Our eyes finally met, and the king had me stunned speechless for a moment.

Clearing my throat, I finally asked, "Yet you kept looking for me? Waiting for me?"

His lips curved upward a bit sadly. "That's the problem with never truly being loved, I guess. It leaves you desperate for it."

My heart swelled, and I nearly stretched across the couch and kissed him. But I needed to clear the rest of the air first. "I was held in a dark prison for my entire life, chained to a wall for every moment except those when I was pulled away and tortured. Even then, the chains remained. I won't tell you details of the torture—I won't allow myself to relive them. But Akari was eighteen when we were captured, and she told me that the horrors we survived were the likes of which she had never imagined."

His expression was so fucking dark, and shadows slipped slowly off his skin, curling into the air around us.

I continued anyway. "They wanted to extract the kings' magic from us, and went to nearly every length they could think of to do so. I was spared from the sexual attacks because of my age, but Akari and Vena..." I trailed off, my magic gathering and my body shuddering with the horror of the memories. The looks in their eyes, the devastation in their sobs...

Fuck, it had been awful.

Twenty-one was the age of maturity for fae, and sexual contact with anyone before that age was even more grievous a crime than killing. So much so that even the monsters who'd held us captive weren't willing to touch me before then.

"The night we escaped, they were going to rape me. We all knew it; tears leaked from Vena's eyes for my sake for days prior. It was my birthday—my torturers sneered so as they pulled me away from Vena and Akari."

Another shudder tore through me.

"You don't have to tell me anything you don't want to, Diora." Namir's voice was fierce, his arms wrapping around me before he dragged me across the couch, turning me and setting me down on his lap. My back rested against his chest, and my breaths came out a bit painfully. His shadows dispelled my monster, though, and that urged me to finish the story.

"I want you to trust me—and I want you to know," I admitted. His arms tightened around me, but the hold was far from uncomfortable. "My monster took over frequently, but she had never turned to full shadow, like you did in the forest that one day. I had no idea that was even possible—and neither did she, apparently. I wonder what would've been different, if I had known, but the wondering does nothing but hurt me more."

My stomach clenched as memories assaulted me, but I continued. "The men who dragged me toward the torture rooms were spewing obscenities, talking about the way they would hurt me as they violated my body. Terror flooded me, and my monster took over. One moment, the chains were around me and the men were dragging me, the next, there was blood everywhere. The men were all dead when she gave the control back to me. My chains were on the floor, and for the first time in my entire life, I was free."

I paused to take a shaky breath in. "Much of what happened next is a blur to me, same with the torture and the trauma. I found the keys to our chains on the men's bodies, and then made my way back to Vena and Akari. My monster took over again when I came across a few more guards, but I tried not to look at their faces or their bodies. When Akari and Vena were free from their chains, Akari took over, and got us out of there. My monster took over a few more times—there was so much blood. Akari killed the last few men, though, and found running water, so we could clean ourselves a bit before we put on the clothing we had stolen off the dead guards. From there, we ran a long way, then stopped at an inn and stayed until we were ready to split up and hunt the kings who had cursed us."

"I'm sorry that didn't happen the way you wanted it to," he murmured, his arms still locked tightly around me.

"Killing you? I'm not. I didn't really know what I wanted before; my only real priority was my freedom. And here, with you, I feel freer than I ever have before." My words were completely and totally honest.

Namir sighed softly. "There's something I have to tell you."

I tried to turn my head a bit toward him, but failed. Was that guilt in his voice?

"My brother—" He cut himself off, his body growing stiff.

"Your brother what?"

I was left on my ass on the couch a moment later, and Namir had turned almost completely to shadows.

"Stay here," he snarled at me. "Laith will be looking for you."

He disappeared through the shadowed barrier that blocked the entrance to his room.

Laith?

He was the Dark King, wasn't he? The cruel one, whose magic Vena possessed?

My stomach clenched, my magic gathering like a knife in my abdomen.

"Oh no," I whispered, dread flooding me as the magic took control—as the monster tore free.

She sprinted after Namir, slipping through the shadowed doors with ease as all hell broke loose in the castle. Some fae were handing out swords while others gave orders. More were ushered into the kitchen; that door was naturally concealed by the stone it was made out of.

Everyone who saw my wolf lunged out of the way, and for the first time, ripping everyone to shreds wasn't her priority.

Instead of killing, she *hunted*.

She streaked out of the castle, and into the city. The air was drenched in shadows, but off in the distance, I could see the darkness warring with them, slowly devouring them. They whispered,

Run.

Run.

Run.

I felt their urgency, and silently encouraged my monster to run faster, to cover more ground.

Namir was somewhere in the forest; I could *feel* it. And that was exactly where my wolf ran, as if she could feel him too.

The shadows grew thicker, dancing erratically around my monster as she flew through the woods. She paid no mind to their stress, pushing forward, toward Namir. And where he was, I knew the Dark King would probably be too.

A burst of darkness broke through a cloud of shadows, devouring a massive chunk of the dark fog whole. With the brothers each possessing one part of the Night Throne's magic, their powers complemented one another evenly. Neither of the men could kill each other—

But Laith could kill me, and I could kill him.

As my monster had proven, she would destroy anything and anyone she needed to in order to survive. If Laith attacked her, he'd find himself facing a fiercer opponent than he expected.

But... neither she nor I had learned how to fight since we'd gotten free of our chains. We'd learned to cook, and make pottery, and mend dresses, and dance the most basic steps, but we hadn't learned to act and react the way a warrior would.

I'd just have to hope that grit was enough to carry us through, I supposed.

The shadows and darkness grew thicker and heavier as my wolf plunged deeper into the forest.

We saw the first fight, then.

A shadow fae I recognized from the castle, one who trained with Namir frequently. She was short but just as well-muscled as the king—and sometimes even faster than him. I saw the shadows leaking off her form as she faced off with a fae whose figure blended into the darkness surrounding them. He'd nearly disappeared, but not completely.

My wolf had one focus: reaching Namir.

Finding her king.

But I urged her toward the female fae, unwilling to let the woman risk her life when my wolf could make her chances of survival so much greater.

For one of the first times in my life, my wolf obeyed me.

She turned fully to shadow, and then lunged toward the battling fae. Her smoke-like form went straight through Namir's friend, and her teeth materialized just in time to tear straight through the large male fae's throat.

His head hit the ground and his body followed quickly.

My wolf landed smoothly, her paws immaterial once again.

The female warrior looked a bit pale, but nodded her thanks toward my wolf before turning and sprinting further into the forest, toward the place the shadows and darkness seemed to be converging.

That would be the place we would find Namir and his brother—that would be the place we fought for the life of my mate.

My wolf began running in the same direction as the other fae, but something made her pause a moment after she started.

Skidding to a stop, she looked around the forest, searching for... something.

I didn't know what she was looking for, but there was this feeling in my chest—this eerie, achy feeling that I didn't understand. It felt foreign, and—

My breathing cut off as darkness flooded my wolf's throat.

The magic I possessed didn't just react; it exploded.

Shadows tore through the darkness, ripping the thick magic from my lungs and giving me an airway again. My wolf gasped for breath but wasted no time, turning jerkily as she searched for the person behind the power.

The darkness was strong—really strong.

But Namir had to have known where his brother was, didn't he? He had warned me that Laith would be looking for me, but...

My thoughts cut off as my eyes collided with a set that were nearly identical to Namir's, but instead of gray, they were pure black.

The man they belonged to was about the same height as my king, with the same naturally tan skin and dark hair, but built entirely differently. Laith's muscles were bulging and chiseled, every inch of his arms and legs much thicker than Namir's. Where Namir was built to run and swing a sword, his brother was built to injure and destroy.

And feeling the intensity of the power that emanated from the man, I realized I understood why Namir had played defense for so long. Nothing about his brother so much as whispered empathy, or love, or compassion.

He was a brute, through and through.

A thick metal sword sliced through the smoke and darkness, toward my wolf, and it took me much longer than it should've to realize that it was headed toward my throat.

CHAPTER 21

MY WOLF WENT immaterial only a moment before the sword should've cut through her.

There was a savage snarl behind her, and Namir's shadowy form cut through hers as he put himself between her and his brother. A loud clanging sound filled the air as the Shadow King's blade collided with the Dark King's, and the brothers began to move together in what I could only call a dance.

Their feet moved rapidly, their bodies spinning and turning and pivoting as they reacted to each other's movements as if they'd done so a million times before—which, I realized, they may have while they were growing up.

"Get back to the castle," Namir snarled, and there was no doubt the words were geared toward me. But my monster was in control, and even as I pushed against her, urging her to leave, she wouldn't walk away from Namir.

More fae burst from the shadows and darkness. Swords clashed, and the metallic scent of blood tinged the air.

My wolf didn't hesitate to join those fights, and with her control over my magic, none of the other fae could stop her.

She wasn't trained, but she moved like the shadows that were a part of her—like the shadows *she* was a part of—materializing in time to tear flesh, bones, and throats, and dematerializing before anyone could tear into her. She wasn't skilled, but she was angry, and brutal, and vicious.

The numbers of dark fae dwindled quickly, the shadow fae retreating as the remaining dark ones swarmed my wolf, focusing on the monster that was decimating their ranks. She didn't respect life the way fae were supposed to—all she cared about was survival, and victory, and protecting the city I was coming to love.

She wasn't my enemy... but she wasn't my ally, either.

When the last of the dark fae around my wolf fell, her eyes landed on the two kings moving unnaturally fast. Their blades clashed again and again, the noise louder than anything I had ever heard from the castle's training room. My monster's gaze could barely keep up with the speed the men moved at.

"Your men have fallen," Namir snarled at his brother. "You saw my female fight. Run while you have the chance."

I didn't know why he considered my monster *his female*, but it wasn't as if I could take over and say that in the middle of the fight.

Laith laughed darkly. "I saw a desperate woman with no control over her magic, and a man too weak to force her to learn. At least dad was man enough to make mother hone her gifts—your female seems to think she's actually become a wolf."

Namir's snarl was furious, and his fury changed his fighting immediately.

He swung his sword harder, and faster, his movements somehow picking up even more speed. His sword sliced at his brother's throat too quickly for Laith to block, but a fraction of a second before the blade would've cut his skin, the dark king dissolved.

His darkness swept out of the forest, leaving us with the thick shadows that resembled smoke or fog.

Laith's words began to set in when Namir spun toward me, his eyes dark and wild, his chest rising and falling as he heaved for breaths.

"Your female seems to think she's actually become a wolf," Laith had said.

Namir hadn't argued, or told Laith he was wrong.

He had called my wolf *his female*.

...He had called *me* his female.

While my monster was in control.

My body began to quiver.

Was Laith right?

Hadn't Namir already said the same thing?

"The way you see it determines how it makes itself known," he'd told Jesh and Lavee on one of those first days in the forest. *"When it comes to magic, almost everything is in your head."*

Stars.

He knew that I thought my magic had a life of its own.

He knew that I thought it was a curse—that it was a monster I couldn't control.

He'd let me continue to believe that.

And I'd been stupid enough, and naïve enough, and desperate enough not to realize it wasn't true until now.

My wolf's head jerked toward the line of shadow fae in the trees.

Toward the solemn looks on their faces—toward the grave looks in their eyes as they surveyed the bodies around my wolf.

No, not my wolf.

The bodies around *me*.

There was no wicked creature within me.

There was no beast waiting to use my emotional moments to break free from the cage in my chest.

There was just me.

Diora.

A freed prisoner, a wolf...

And a monster.

A murderer.

The wall between my "wolf" and myself dissolved. I remained in the wolf's shape, but the defenses I'd used to separate myself from her turned to dust.

And all I felt?

Fear.

Fear so thick it made my eyes water.

Namir stepped toward me, his hands out in front of him. His sword was on the dirt behind him, abandoned and forgotten. "Diora, Love," he said, his voice low and gravelly, but soft too somehow.

I wanted to shift, to snarl at him that he didn't love me. That he'd lost the right to call me that when he decided not to tell me what he'd clearly realized long before that day.

But his warriors were still in the trees, staring at me like...
well, like I'd murdered a dozen dark fae.

And I had.

So, shoving away my fury, I gave in to my panic, and ran.

My paws carried me into the forest quickly—faster than I'd
ever realized I could move. And as I ran, it occurred to me
that they didn't feel like paws.

They felt like feet.

My feet.

I had dissolved into the shadows, reforming into a wolf, but I
was still me when I was in that form.

And the feeling that accompanied that knowledge gutted me.

Namir was behind me; I could hear him behind me. And
based on the way I'd seen him move earlier, there was no
question in my mind whether or not he could run faster
than me.

He had lied to me.

Not outright—he'd never spoken about my monster, that I
could remember. And he'd never said that he *couldn't* move
faster than your average fae, either.

But he hadn't told me those things.

And to me, that was as good as a lie.

I ran until my lungs burned too much to keep running, until my legs shook so hard that I could no longer continue. My knees cracked against each other, and I went down hard.

Namir caught me before my face met the rocky dirt below me—his hand was on my bicep, and he lowered me to the ground when he realized I couldn't stand anymore.

My face was coated in dried blood that flaked off my skin with every brush of a tree branch or hand. Tear stains tracked down my cheeks, cutting through the cracked crimson that was evidence of the lives I'd taken.

Not my wolf.

Not my monster.

Me.

I had taken those lives; I had killed those fae.

I belonged on the sunny island, where my magic would be voided and I'd slowly die a horrible, painful death.

But Namir would never take me there; he never took anyone there.

"Let go of me." I ripped my arm away from him, as soon as my legs were on the dirt, my body kneeling in front of him unintentionally.

He dropped to his knees in front of me, his hands capturing mine. The look in his eyes was desperate, and panicked.

It only infuriated me further.

He knew he hadn't been honest.

"What else have you kept from me?" I snarled at the king.

Unlike me, he wasn't drenched in blood. There were a few cuts on his torso, but they were already healed—he must've healed faster than most fae, too, because it was too soon to be completely recovered. I was more acquainted with the healing times for various wounds than most fae—far more acquainted.

"Diora." His voice had an edge of desperation, but also growl. "I was trying to protect you—I've always been trying to protect you."

"I never asked you to do that." My glower was hot and fierce. "Tell me *now*."

He shoved a hand through his hair. It was the first time I'd seen him like that—scared, and angry, and unhinged. "Now that we've met, our lives are connected. We'll live or die as one, whether or not the bond begins to fully form. Laith knows, which means he'll be focused on doing everything he can to kill you, to end me. He can't kill me, because we share magic—but you aren't connected to him. Only me. We need to cement the bond."

"Like hell we do," I snarled back. "You'll never fucking touch me again."

His gaze grew darker, and more desperate. "You're in danger, Diora."

"I've been in danger since the day I was born."

"You're *vulnerable*."

My glare heated. "Because I wasn't while I was chained to a wall for twenty-one fucking years? Vulnerability is nothing new to me. I'd prefer risking my life daily to being bonded with a bastard who'd lie to me about my own magic. What else have you kept to yourself?"

His expression only grew darker. "Nothing."

I barked out a humorless laugh. "Like hell you haven't."

My finger lifted, my hand and arm shaking as I pointed toward the castle I'd finally started to think of as my home.

That was over, now.

"Go back to your fucking castle, King Namir. Whatever we were is over. I don't give people second chances; not even my damned fated mate." My magic was gathering in my abdomen again, but this time, it wasn't with fear—it was with fury.

Hatred.

Sadness.

And when it burst, there wouldn't be a wolf.

There would just be me, and the shadows that seemed to have consumed my soul.

His eyes burned into me, the shadows in them nearly black. "I won't leave you."

"Yes, you will." The magic that had gathered within me exploded, and for once in my life, I welcomed it.

The shadows erupted from my abdomen, from my skin, from my veins. The air was thick, and sharp, and furious, the magic gathered around me in a thick sphere of swirling, hissing power.

They would keep Namir out—keep him away.

The sphere stretched wider, my head tilting back and my arms spreading wide as the power poured off of me. I didn't know how much I possessed, or how much damage I could do, but I knew that Namir's shadows danced through every part of the forest that surrounded his city, protecting it and apparently alerting him when his brother tried to get in.

If his magic was that vast, so was mine.

He'd said before that he only possessed the throne's power, and that my connection to the shadows was different than his own.

Different enough to keep him away from me, I hoped.

There were no markings on my throat; our bond hadn't actually formed. I didn't know what would set that in action, but it wasn't as if I could ask Namir.

He'd only tell me half the truth.

The wall of shadows I'd created continued spreading and stretching, pushing Namir with it. The king didn't break through, though I could feel him fighting my magic, trying to cut through my shadows.

He couldn't, though.

I was still free.

Not completely, but... free enough.

CHAPTER 22

NAMIR

I COLLIDED with a tree hard enough to break a lesser fae's back, then crashed to the ground too quickly for my shadows to catch me.

I deserved the pain, though.

Diora's words had killed me—and they had killed me because I knew she was right.

I should've trusted her sooner.

I should've confided in her earlier.

I should've warned her that Laith would be coming after her, that her "monster" was just her mind and body's way of protecting itself, that things weren't always going to be as easy as they had seemed.

Since we'd met, I'd been trying to protect her. And I would never stop doing so—but I had gone about it the wrong way, that was for fucking sure.

I'd wanted to give her the life she dreamed of, where she could become a chef or a seamstress or a ceramicist, or whatever it was that she liked. I'd wanted her to live out her days safely and happily. I'd wanted her to have everything she could possibly imagine—to live a life filled with peace, and safety, and security.

But it was clear, now, that what I wanted for her wasn't an option.

And even more, that it might not be what *she* wanted at all.

I'd tried so hard to keep our conversations playful and fun. To make her smile, to make her laugh. To make her happy. And I thought I had succeeded.

But she didn't just want happiness—she wanted our relationship to have depth. She wanted to understand my past, and to help me understand hers.

I hadn't realized that, and in my obliviousness, I may have well and truly fucked myself over.

Shoving that idea away, I finally peeled myself off the dirt.

I was the king, for fuck's sake; I couldn't just throw in the towel because I'd screwed things up so damned epically with my female.

I ignored the blood drying over a couple of my almost-healed wounds as I strode toward the edge of the shadowed wall. My hands skimmed the surface of the structure, and I grew more impressed by the moment as my own shadows slid around the shield Diora had built around herself.

That thing was fucking sturdy.

I considered trying to break into it, but shot that idea down almost instantly.

Diora was furious with me, and if I broke down the wall she'd built to protect herself, she would only be more livid—and more hurt by my actions.

I didn't think what I'd done was necessarily wrong; I had only been doing what I thought was best for her. I sure as fuck hadn't been holding back out of cruelty.

But she was still hurting because of it, and I had to take responsibility for that.

My gaze skimmed the area around me, my shadows still working their way around Diora's shelter, following her walls and wrapping around them lightly enough that she wouldn't notice my power strengthening hers, keeping her safe.

She needed time, and space, and I would give that to her.

My eyes landed on the log of a tree that looked like it had tipped over a decade earlier, and I strode over to it. My shadows were still moving, but they were doing so out of my sight and Diora's as well.

Now, I just needed to check my wounds... and then wait.

Jesh, Lavee, and a few of my other warriors came jogging out of the forest, looking as if they hadn't even been in a damned battle at all. Diora was to blame for that—and I was fucking proud of her for it.

She had been a one-woman army out there, ferocious, deadly, and absolutely beautiful.

Her wolf form was so damned incredible, I was almost tempted to try one out myself.

"Way to screw things the fuck up," Jesh growled at me, as he and the others slowed.

"What are you going to do now?" Lavee changed the subject before another fight broke out. I was exhausted after facing off with Laith, but not exhausted enough that I wouldn't defend myself, or my mate.

"Wait until she's ready to come out." I turned my face toward her shadowed wall, still musing silently about how damned incredible her control over her magic was.

She didn't even fucking know it, but she had more skill with the shadows than anyone I'd ever seen—myself included. With a little practice, she would surpass me easily, and I'd only be even more attracted to her for it.

Jesh drawled, "I'm sure she'll appreciate that."

Lavee grabbed a rock off the ground and threw it at his head half-heartedly. The other warriors exchanged snorts and grins, but my gaze went back to Diora's wall.

"Jesh will get the tent," Lav announced, striding over and plopping down on the log beside me.

"Like fuck he will," Jesh grumbled.

"I won't sleep in a tent. She's alone in the forest, under the stars, so I will be too," I told them all, my gaze remaining firmly in place. "I failed her; I won't live in a damned tent while she's roughing it because of me."

There was a beat of silence.

"Well, I'm going back to the castle," Jesh told me.

Lav snorted. "Of course you are."

He growled at her, but strode away a moment later.

A few others sat down on the log beside me. Soon, we would need to coordinate a crew to bury the bodies of Laith's people, to make sure that our forest was clear and taken care of. We'd need to check on our own people, too, and mourn any that Laith's had injured or killed.

But for the moment, we all just sat there silently.

"You'd be a fool not to fight for her," Lav said to me after a few minutes, her voice low and quiet. "She'll be furious—but afraid even more than that."

"I know." My voice was simple, but I didn't leave any question behind the words. Lav and Diora were friends, but Diora and I were much, much more. We'd spent hours upon hours together in my room as I taught her to read and write, and in her bed as we got to know each other's bodies. We'd traded jokes, and stories. Though most of the stories had been mine, she had spent a few small, good moments with her sisters that she had shared with me, and I relished every tiny detail she gave me. "I'll grovel if I have to; she's mine, and I'm hers."

Lav dipped her head in a nod. "You're a good man, even if you've been kind of a shitty mate."

I snorted. "Thanks, Lav."

"Any time." She winked at me, and then both of us focused our eyes on Diora's shield.

My mate would emerge eventually—and then I'd do whatever the fuck it took to get her back in my arms, in my life, and in my bed.

Chapter 23

Diora

A few days passed. There was a stream of fresh water within the large, safe sphere that I was holding to separate myself from Namir, so I used it to wash and drink. The strain of the magic grew easier as the days passed, and I stretched the power out further to test myself as I stayed away from the king.

The space between us helped me think clearer, and gave me time to work through the horrors I had committed. The things I'd done were unforgivable, but they hadn't been pointless or unreasonable. I had killed to protect myself when my friends and I escaped the prison, not out of hatred —though I did hate them. Had I left them alive, they would've been hunting me.

My captors, the ones who had been in charge of the prison, were likely still searching for me, Vena, and Akari, but I didn't fear them any longer. I'd been wild and confused and afraid back then, and I hadn't understood my magic. Now that I did, there was no cage that could hold me. There was no prison that could trap me, and no jailer that could hurt me.

I commanded the shadows, and they answered to me.

Not their king; not any of his brothers, either.

Me.

I had no desire to be queen, but knowing that I was stronger, that the shadows were mine, made me feel free in a way nothing else had.

Not even their king.

It hadn't felt like it before, when I was furious at Namir in the forest, but I had many options. Too many, even.

I could waltz back into the castle and declare myself the city's queen. But as I'd established, I didn't want that.

I could leave. Now that I was starting to understand my shadows, I knew that I could make myself dissolve into them. Doing so, I could get away from Namir without leaving any kind of a trail.

If I wanted to, I could go to Laith's city. I could search for Vena, and warn her away from the bastard king she was connected to, if not fated to be with also. Or I could go to the Night King's court, and warn Akari away from him. With my control over my magic, I felt sure that I could safely find my friends, one way or another.

But I wasn't sure I wanted to do any of those things.

Vena and Akari had never looked at me like I was a monster, but they also hadn't told me that I wasn't actually shifting forms or being possessed. Akari, at least, had to have known the truth.

I'd started becoming a wolf during the most painful moments of my life as a child; I was sure that they'd kept the secret from me because they saw it as a coping mechanism, or a way for me to survive. But they didn't know how much I had feared that part of myself, or just how difficult it had been for me to feel like I had no control in that way.

So I wasn't ready to go looking for them. Not yet.

It would've also been possible for me to slip out of the city and try to find a completely random place to live, and to establish myself there. I could begin training as a chef, or a dancer. There, I could live a life I'd never even fantasized about, because it was so simple and beautiful.

But... I wasn't sure I wanted to do that, either.

So I remained in the forest, hoping something would happen to suddenly help me decide what I wanted to do with myself, and my life.

I'd been there five days, and was leaning over the stream to get some water when a bit of movement a good distance to my right caught my attention. It was probably just an animal in the forest outside my shadowed protection, but I wanted to check anyway.

Standing up, I strode across the distance between my stream and the edge of my shadowed barrier.

The shadows thinned as I approached, requiring no command. As Namir had said, they were an extension of me. And as long as I saw them that way, they would mold themselves to my will, moving and changing as I willed them to.

My eyebrows lifted when I found Lavee leaned up against a tree outside my barrier, tossing a small knife in the air repeatedly, and catching it as it fell down.

I scanned the trees behind her, looking for any sign of Namir. It definitely wouldn't be past him to use her as bait to convince me to open up the boundaries of my shadowed barrier.

But, I could always just replace it and kick him out if he did so.

So, I parted the shadows, stepping into the doorway I'd created in the shield and then leaning up against one side of them.

Lavee's gaze trailed over the gap in my shadows. "Damn, Diora."

"Did he send you?" I didn't bother beating around the bush.

"No. He's made it clear to all of us that he wants us to leave you alone until you're ready to come out."

My gaze scanned the forest.

I believed her... mostly.

Namir had broken my trust, and that made it hard to trust any of his friends.

"So, are you just going to stay out here forever?" She gestured toward my shadowed bubble. "Shit in the forest and eat wild mushrooms and bulbs for the rest of your immortal life?"

I scowled. "No. This is temporary; I'm staying until I've decided where I'm going to go next and what I'm going to do."

Understanding softened her face, and she dipped her head, slipping the small knife she'd been flipping into some kind of holster on her thigh, under the slit on her black slip-dress. "What are you considering?"

I shrugged my shoulders, not wanting to tell her.

"Can I come in?" She gestured to my bubble.

I grimaced, and she flashed me a grin as she stepped away from the tree, and then slipped into the space I'd claimed as mine. I didn't mind letting her in, but Namir or Jesh would eventually come looking for her, and they'd both broken my trust already.

"Not much, huh?" Her gaze swept the shitty bed I'd made myself with moss and soft leaves.

"Nope. But it's temporary." I sat down in the spot I liked to sit in the most, with my back against a smooth tree trunk. She sat on a log I'd set up for preparing food. There wasn't much I could do with the plants I scavenged, but I tried to cut them and toss them together to improve the taste slightly.

Lavee nodded, still looking around. "Namir's kind of a mess out there, you know. He's refused to leave the forest or sleep in a bed or eat normal food since you came out here."

I scowled. "He kept things from me. Big, important things. And he knows honesty is important to me; he just chose not to tell me."

"I don't judge you for feeling that way. I just thought you might like to know that he's fucked up over it too."

Strangely enough, she was right.

I did like knowing that.

If it made me a monster, she could add it to the list.

"Thank you."

She nodded again.

We were both silent for a few minutes, and my eyes closed. The shadows danced slowly around us, murmuring softly and unhappily as they spoke around my pain.

"Can you hear them whisper?" I asked to Lavee after a bit of time had passed, opening my eyes. "The shadows, I mean."

She shook her head, and her gaze grew a bit wistful. "Sometimes I feel the darkness warm, and welcome me. It draws me in, calling me home. But my magic is of Laith's variety, not yours."

Hmm.

The way she felt her magic was kind of intriguing.

"What about Jesh?"

She shrugged. "We don't talk about our magic together. I don't remember the last time we discussed anything other than Namir, honestly. I just can't take the pain."

Her words made me hurt for her. "I'm sorry."

"As am I." She gave me a ghost of a smile, before tilting her head back against the trunk and closing her eyes. "I see why you came here. It's peaceful, and quiet, and safe."

My heart squeezed at that. "It's nice, isn't it?"

"Yes." She paused. "Other than the part where you've got to shit in the forest."

I snorted. "I've shit in much worse places."

A laugh shook her shoulders. "I believe you."

My lips were curved upward as I stared out at the trees in front of me.

We had just joked about my time in prison. I'd never done that—not once, in my entire life. Vena, Akari, and I had helped each other survive, but we hadn't been living. We hadn't been laughing. We hadn't been... enjoying.

But I enjoyed Lavee's company.

And I had really enjoyed Namir's, while that had lasted.

"I think he really was trying to protect you, if that means anything," she added a few minutes later, though her voice was quieter.

"I know." My arms wrapped slowly around my abdomen. "But that doesn't change what he did."

"It doesn't," she admitted.

More silence followed the agreement, until Lavee broke it again.

"What are you considering, for your future? A place in the circus? Think of all the name possibilities for a woman who can turn into a shadow wolf. Shady Lady. Smoke Poke. Shadow... shit, what rhymes shadow? Baddow?"

"That's definitely not a word," I said, with a snort.

She flashed me a grin. "Shadow Baddow it is."

I couldn't help but laugh, and it felt good to do so. "I'm not joining a circus. I've thought about going after my friends who were in prison with me—Vena and Akari. We didn't know anything about the kings, but Vena was going after

Laith, so she's probably in danger. Though, she possesses his magic, so he can't kill her."

Lavee nodded. "A trip into the dark city? That could be fun."

I shrugged. "Could be. I'm also considering just... leaving."

Lavee blinked at me.

"I can turn to shadow, now. Even Namir couldn't track me, I don't think. Leaving the city and finding a new place to live where I can just be a seamstress or something sounds nice. A fresh start would be incredible," I admitted.

"Damn, girl."

I sighed. "I know. It's crazy, right? I'm a monster, it's not like I can just move away from my problems. But stars, it sounds appealing."

She scoffed at me. "You're not a monster; you're a powerful woman who has been through hell and came out both sane and strong. You've never killed anyone who wasn't a threat to your life, have you?"

I grimaced. "No."

Lavee tossed a hand toward me. "Then as far as I'm concerned, you're a hero."

"You didn't see the way Namir's warriors were looking at me in the forest." I shuddered. "Some of Laith's fae would've surrendered. They didn't all need to die."

"Maybe they would've, maybe not." Lavee shrugged. "But I *was* one of Namir's warriors in that forest, and what most of us were looking at you with was awe, Diora. Not anything negative. We've all seen you wolf out before, but none of us have ever seen anyone fight so savagely. It was fucking incredible. And on top of the awe, we were pretty sore-assed, because you saved some of our lives with all those damned shadows that you haven't trained to control, and most of us can barely wrap our swords with the magic in our veins after decades of training."

I rolled my eyes. "That's because Namir's training you."

"Right?" She flashed me a grin. "If I have to hear him tell me again that if I think my magic is a hand, it'll move like a hand, I'm going to stab someone. Probably him."

I snorted. "I wouldn't blame you, or stop you. He seems to heal damn near instantly, anyway, so it's not like his life would be at risk."

She nodded. "Did he not tell you about the strengthened senses and abilities that come with the throne's magic?"

I scowled. "No."

Lavee sighed. "Bastard."

"Yup."

CHAPTER 24

SHE PULLED her small knife from the sheath on her thigh, and started flipping it again, slowly. She seemed to be able to do so without even thinking about it, which was pretty damn impressive to me. I'd probably slice my hand off if I tried that.

"He's faster than most people, and stronger too. Not just magically, but physically. He heals quicker on top of that, and has sort of a sixth sense whenever someone nearby is in danger. That last one might be related to the shadows though; he's pretty close-lipped about everything, as you've probably realized."

"He makes you feel like you're the most important person in the world, but it's a lie," I growled. "He'll keep things from you, and withhold information you deserve to know, acting like everything is fine and dandy and perfect. How much else was a lie?"

"He's a king, Diora, and a good one at that. I agree that he should've told you the truth, but making everyone feel like they're the most important person in the world while he's talking to them is part of the role he plays to keep the peace in the kingdom. That's the reason people love him."

"I thought I was more than that to him. Just another one of his subjects." A scowl twisted my lips further, my anger growing thicker in my chest.

"How would you teach me magic, if you were in charge?" Lavee asked. The subject change was swift, but not entirely shocking given our discussion a few minutes earlier.

"I don't know. I don't even really understand it."

She nodded. "I don't know that anyone does, except possibly Namir. Just humor me.

I sighed. "Fine. Give me a moment."

Closing my eyes, I tapped into the magic swirling in my chest. It was reactive and wild to the extent where I had literally thought it was a life of its own. It was the most emotional part of me—not a hand, but an entirely different piece of my body and soul.

"Close your eyes," I told Lavee, opening mine.

She dutifully did so.

"Put your hands on the dirt, and toss your knife a few feet away." That part was just so she could get lost in her emotions more, but she did so without complaint too.

"I'm teaching you the way I feel my magic, so it might not work," I warned.

"Shut up and teach me already."

I snorted, and her lips curved in a grin.

"No grinning," I chided.

Her grin vanished, though I saw her lips twitch, and rolled my eyes a bit.

This part might hurt her, but she had asked me to teach her. And my magic only really showed itself when I was feeling like shit.

"Think back to the moment you realized that Jesh was your fated mate," I said, quietly.

She had never told me about that moment, but I could imagine it was an emotional one.

All signs of her grin were gone. "Hit me right where it hurts, why don't you," she grumbled at me.

"Shut up and learn already," I teased her softly, reflecting her words to me.

She sighed, but nodded her head.

"Think back to the emotions you felt that day. Excitement, maybe. Dread, perhaps. Everything probably felt a bit overwhelming, but I imagine that at first, you felt at least a little bit hopeful."

Her expression shifted slightly.

I used my magic to wrap her slowly and thinly in shadows, to begin thickening the tension she would theoretically begin to feel in a few moments.

"Now, I want you to imagine that tonight, you're walking up to his room," I said, my voice low. "You want to discuss it again—the mate bond. Your fist raps against his door once, and then again. A moment passes, and you hear giggling. Feminine giggling."

I saw her shoulders tense.

Mates were possessive, even without having a true bond formed.

"A woman answers the door, wrapped in Jesh's bathrobe, with the sleeve falling off her shoulder and one of her breasts practically hanging out. Her hair is tangled, and she's breathing quickly, as if she just slid out of bed after a proper fucking—and the room reeks of sex."

Lavee's nostrils flared as I worked my shadows to whisper words of his unfaithfulness to her. She couldn't hear their whispers, but something told me she still *felt* them.

A shudder tore through her spine.

"What do you feel, Lav?" I asked, my voice still low.

"Fury," she gritted out.

"And?"

"Hatred."

"What else?" I prodded.

"Fear," she snarled.

"Find those emotions in the center of your chest," I instructed. "They'll feel like something living, and growing, and moving."

Her breathing picked up. "Fuck, you're right."

"That's your magic, Lav. It's not a hand; it's what you feel. Embrace it. Let it loose, and let it breathe. You won't hurt me."

My shadows would protect me—but I stood swiftly and strode away from her, giving her more space anyway.

Lavee's body shuddered and shook for a few long, tense moments.

I got ready to walk back over to her, to make sure she was okay, but before I moved, darkness erupted in the shadowy bubble I'd created.

Her magic engulfed the clearing, making everything but my shadows vanish before my eyes. I didn't fear this darkness, though—I could feel in it what she'd said she felt at times.

Warmth.

Welcoming.

It felt like a soft smile, or a gentle breeze.

My eyes closed, and I relished the feel of her magic. Of her emotions.

Not a monster; not a bad thing, or an evil one.

A part of her.

Just like mine was a part of me.

The darkness vanished a moment later, and I opened my eyes to a shocked Lavee staring at me.

"Holy fuck," she crowed, breathing heavily. "Fuckity fuck. Did you see that, Diora? Did you fucking see that?"

"You embraced your power," I said, flashing her a grin.

"I made this whole damn shadowy fishbowl dark! Shit, I'm powerful!" Her exclamations made me laugh.

"Hell yeah, you are."

I felt something sharp hit one side of my *shadowy fishbowl* as Lavee had called it, and winced at the pressure. It eased up for a moment, and then hit me again, harder, and I felt whatever it was cut through my shadowed wall.

I nearly flew across the clearing at the sharpness of the hit, but a muscular arm caught me before I could crash into anything.

My face collided with a warm, bare chest, and the scent in my nostrils told me exactly who it was.

I jerked away from him, despite the longing in my body to throw my arms around Namir and hug him fiercely. His hand remained locked tightly around my bicep, though.

"Was that you?" I growled at him.

His eyes were soft but wary as they scanned the space around us, searching for threats, and I was a bit stunned to see the thick circles beneath them, declaring his exhaustion.

Had he really been living out in the forest, eating plants, just like me?

"What the hell was that, Diora?" he finally asked. "I felt darkness—an assload of darkness."

"That was me." Lavee was still grinning massively, her shoulders and arms wiggling a bit as she did a little dance. I bit back a snort, attempting to tug my arm away from Namir's grip.

He still didn't release me, though his grip also wasn't tight enough to cause pain.

"That can't have been you." Jesh frowned, a few feet away from the rest of us. His arms were folded over his chest, his expression critical. "I could feel that, and I've never felt your magic before. And if anyone could, it would be me."

"Probably because you're an idiot," I shot back.

Lavee snorted, crossing the distance between us to high-five me. "That was a terrible burn, but I'm proud of you anyway."

We exchanged devious grins.

There was something between suspicion and horror in both of the men's eyes.

"What happened?" Namir growled at me.

"Diora taught me how to access my magic. Turns out your hand lessons weren't as useful as I thought." She shrugged, stepping back. Her eyes closed, and I watched in fascination as darkness rippled over her skin, slowly covering every inch of her until she'd nearly vanished.

Her skin rematerialized a moment later, her chest rising and falling rapidly as she grinned my way.

"It'll get easier," I promised her, trying again to tug my arm away from Namir.

Once again, I was unsuccessful.

"It feels like the magic is sort of resisting me," she said, frowning my way.

I nodded. "It's you and the magic both, I think. You'll have to get used to leaning into that power instead of avoiding it, and it'll take some time, but you'll be able to stretch it further and use more of it the more you practice."

She stretched her arms and shoulders out a bit, wiggling her fingers and head as she tapped into her magic again. Darkness leaked from her fingertips, her eyes narrowing as she watched the light leach itself from the world around her.

Jesh stared at her so intensely I nearly fanned myself.

"Stars," Namir murmured, watching his friend use more magic than he'd probably realized she could. "What did you tell her?"

He didn't have to nudge me or use my name for me to know he was addressing me.

"I taught her what magic truly is. Which you should've taught me." I tried yet again to free my arm from his grip, but his fingers only tightened. "Let me go, bastard."

"Not until you've had a conversation with me." For once, his voice wasn't playful. It wasn't angry or cruel either, though.

I growled back, "You knew there was no monster within me, and you let me talk about it like a fool. We have nothing to discuss, Namir. Release my arm, and go back to your damned castle."

"You were *never* a fool." His words were sharp, and his shadows wrapped around us, separating us from Jesh and Lavee. His hand remained around my bicep, and he stepped around to the front of me so our eyes collided.

His were dark, and the emotions in his eyes had me growing quiet. "What was I supposed to say to you, Diora? You had just gotten free, and you were so scared of me and yourself that you were living in the forest rather than the castle. I couldn't tell you that you were your own monster; that would've crushed you. I intended to explain everything as soon as you decided to train with me, I swear."

"And if I'd never decided to train with you?" I asked, my voice shaking a bit.

"Then why the hell would you ever need to know? Some things are better left undiscovered, Love."

"You don't get to decide those things for me," I shot back, though I knew my argument was weak, and weakening by the moment. "And you don't get to call me *Love*. Not anymore."

His lips curved upward slightly, a bit of that soft playfulness that I loved returning to his eyes. When he was genuinely teasing me for the fun of it, he was nearly impossible for me to resist. "And how will you respond if I do, *Love*?"

Damn him.

Damn him to the damned stars.

"Drop your shadows, or I'll drop them for you," I said, my voice harsh. "This conversation is over."

His other hand lifted to rest on my cheek.

For some ridiculous reason, I didn't shove it away.

"Tell me honestly what would've happened had I admitted to you on day one that you were the monster you feared, Diora. Tell me how that conversation would've gone down differently than I imagine it, and I will step back and give you as much space as you want."

Damn him.

I tried to imagine myself, back in the forest.

He was right; I'd been terrified.

So, so terrified.

And those first few days in the castle... stars, I was an uncertain mess.

His lips lifted the tiniest bit. "I won't push you to let me share your bed again, but please come back to the castle. Let me teach you how to fight with a sword, not just your teeth. I'd feel a hell of a lot better if you could protect yourself... and maybe you can do for my warriors the same thing you did for Lav?" He gestured with his head, toward the place she had been standing.

I sighed.

I could be hard-headed, but I did know when I'd been beat, and Namir had practically demolished my argument in this situation.

So, I agreed.

CHAPTER 25

AFTER AN EXTREMELY LONG WALK BACK TO the castle, during which Lavee never stopped practicing her magic, and the shadows continuously whispered seductive words about how Namir felt like home, and love, and comfort, we finally made it back.

I needed a shower, badly, so I locked myself in my room. Namir was probably waiting outside the door, I knew, but I still wasn't sure whether or not I was ready to forgive him.

And even if I was ready to forgive him, I wasn't ready to take our relationship back to where we'd been. The night of the attack, I had been planning on staying in Namir's room. Sleeping with him there—maybe even having sex with him there, consequences be damned.

I had felt... whole.

Now, I just felt confused.

Should I move on?

Try to completely forget everything that had happened over the past week?

Forgive Namir, and move on?

I wasn't sure.

So I took my time in the shower, washing all the dirt and emotions down the drain until I felt refreshed, invigorated, and focused.

I'd worry about Namir another time—for now, I would focus on training.

Learning how to survive.

When I could no longer avoid reality beneath the hot running water, I slipped into my closet and took my time going through every one of my dresses. I didn't recognize any of them, and they were even more intricate and fancy than I remembered—people must've still been crafting clothing for me after my fight in the forest.

I wasn't sure how I felt about that, and wasn't ready to look more closely at those feelings, either.

Choosing one of the outfits that wasn't the fanciest or the plainest, I slipped into my clothing and smoothed the fabric down my thighs. There was a slit going up one leg, leaving room for me to move, which I assumed I'd need if I was going to learn to fight. I could always ask for a pair of pants to wear instead, but if I wanted to be ready for a fight at any time, I'd need to train in a skirt.

Plus, I liked my dresses.

I reluctantly made my way into my bathroom and grabbed a comb off the counter, working it through the tangles in my hair. Despite the usefulness of the training that was coming, I wasn't excited to spend that much time with Namir.

A knock at the door was followed by a call of, "Where are you, Shadow Lady?"

My lips curved upward a bit.

Lavee.

"I'll braid your hair, so you can fight without getting it chopped off," she added from the hallway.

I crossed the room and tugged the door open. My shoulders went back a bit when I saw Namir leaned up against the wall beside the door, but he didn't try to push his way into the room.

"I still need you to teach me how to do the fancy braids," I told her, waving her into the room.

My golden eyes met Namir's gorgeous shadowed grays for a moment, and I hesitated.

He hadn't had the chance to shower, so he was still coated in dirt, and the lines under his eyes were thick and dark.

He flashed me a small smile anyway.

"Go shower," I told him, quietly. "Take a nap."

"I'm not leaving you." His eyes remained locked on mine.

"It's right downstairs." I gestured toward the stairs.

"I've been worried about you for days, Diora. I can finally see you and hear you again; I'm not walking away now."

I sighed. "Lav can do my hair in the bedroom, you can shower in here. Come on, possessive bastard." I held the door open.

He didn't budge. "I'm fine, Love. Go get your hair done."

Another sigh nearly escaped me, but I held it back.

Namir had withheld information from me, things that he should've told me.

But his intentions hadn't been bad.

Not even a little.

And as much as I wished it didn't, that mattered to me.

"Do you still want to talk?" I asked him.

I heard the honesty in his voice as he murmured, "More than almost anything."

"After training, we'll meet in your room. Find me chocolate beforehand, and I'll even try to have a good attitude about it."

His lips curved upward just the tiniest bit. "Is that a promise?"

"Nope." I mirrored his small smile before stepping back into the room, closing the door behind me.

"Think you're going to work things out?" Lavee asked me, as I made it into the bathroom.

"I don't know. He wasn't trying to hurt me, I don't think. He was protecting me the way he thought I needed to be protected. I appreciate that he wanted me to feel safe and secure, that he wanted me to explore the city and learn new things freely. But..." I shrugged.

"But he still kept things from you." Her hip rested against the stone of the countertop. "Honestly, I didn't realize that you weren't aware that the wolf was you. I don't think Jesh did, either. Not that we talk when Namir isn't around, but he seemed surprised when you got angry with the king. So I don't think he knew."

I shrugged. "I don't particularly care what Jesh thinks or knows. He and I are not friends."

Lavee's eyebrows shot upward as she stepped up behind me. "What did he do to you?"

"On the first day we met, he asked me about my scars. I trusted him with an answer, and he told Namir."

She whistled. "Bastard."

"I know. I'm sure everyone was curious about me, but all I really have is trust at this point. That was especially true back then, which is why I would've rather had the truth from the start. I'm not sure how I would've reacted to it, but that doesn't prevent me from wishing I'd known."

Her fingers tugged and wove through my hair as she worked the wet strands quickly. "I don't blame you for that. But... we're all just people. We make mistakes. I'm on your side in this, not Namir's, but it seems like he was trying to respect your wishes to avoid violence and magic and training and whatnot."

I sighed. "I know. Everything would be much easier if I didn't know, but I do. We're going to talk after training."

She snorted. "I'll bet you a dozen gold that all you do after training is sleep."

I rolled my eyes at her. "You know no one's ever given me gold, Lav."

Her lips split in a grin. "Then you'd have to get a job and work for it, so I'll double the bet."

"Fine, fine. I'll bet the gold that I can stay awake just fine after training, so Namir and I can talk."

"And when you fall asleep before you ever get to chat, you'll owe me." She winked at me, and I scowled.

"Not a damn chance."

She finished my hair up a few minutes later, and we slipped out of my room. Namir was still in the hallway, still wearing the same pair of pants, still messy and dirty.

I'd thought he was going to take a shower, not sit outside while the dirt continued soaking into his skin.

A sigh escaped me.

He really wasn't going to wash up unless I went down to his room with him, was he?

That gave me only one choice, I supposed.

"We'll meet you there in a few minutes," I told Lavee, grabbing Namir's arm and steering him toward his room as we reached the bottom of the stairs together. "The king needs to change, and deodorize."

She snorted. "Yes ma'am."

After a quick wink, she headed for the training room while Namir and I strode through the thick shadows at the entrance to his space. The shadows closed behind us, leaving us alone together.

"Are you telling me I stink, female?" The king's voice was playful, and genuine.

"Yes." I tossed him a scowl. "You shouldn't have stayed in the forest for so long."

"You shouldn't have either."

Our gazes were locked, both of us serious and slightly angry.

I finally looked away, tossing a hand toward the bathroom. "Wash up, so we can start training. Stars know I'm going to need it."

He slipped away from me, wispy shadows rippling through the air after him as he headed into the bathroom.

There was no way he was actively making them do that, which meant he was probably a little out of control. Or if not out of control, then just...

Reacting?

Wild?

Tired?

I wasn't sure what was going on with him honestly, but I had never seen his shadows moving without him directly using them before.

My gaze lingered after him.

Something was wrong with him, or for him.

We had disagreed, but that didn't mean I wanted him hurting.

He was still my friend, and he was still my mate.

So I strode into the bathroom after him, just as he stepped inside the shower, completely naked. There was no door to his shower, just an opening and a fancy-looking slab of rock separating the shower from the rest of the bathroom.

My eyes tracked his ass; it was tight, and strong, and really fucking sexy.

I still hadn't seen him naked, and the urge to do so hit me hard in that moment.

Pushing it away, I stepped up to the opening in the shower. Namir faced away from me, his gorgeous ass staring shamelessly at me.

I stretched my shadows toward him, filling the air lightly to let him know I was there.

His muscles relaxed when my shadows slid over his skin, his head tilting back as the water rained down on his face.

Stars, he was beautiful.

And I had missed him, I realized.

That was big for me.

Really, really big.

I had never missed anyone before; I'd never had anyone *to* miss. My relationship with Vena and Akari was strange because we had been connected through our pain. And I hoped we would reconnect in our joy or happiness, after our year apart had passed. But I didn't miss them.

Yet after just a few days, I had missed Namir.

I'd missed his jokes, his laughter. His grins. Even his practiced smiles.

He wasn't putting them on his face to be cruel; he was just doing his job, as the king.

And he was really damn good at that job.

His people loved him, and I...

Fuck.

Did I love him too?

My throat swelled.

I had missed him. I was angry at him, and I still felt a bit frustrated by what he hadn't told me. But despite that anger, I couldn't actually see myself leaving him permanently, or hating him permanently.

Or even really disliking him.

He was my mate, and he had protected me in exactly the way he thought I needed to be protected.

And I hated to admit it, but honestly, he hadn't been wrong. I didn't know what would've happened if he'd told me that I was the monster I feared so much in those first days in the forest, but I knew it wouldn't have been good.

It could've destroyed me.

And he had protected me from that, whether I liked it or not.

I opened my mouth to say all that, to spill those emotions, but the words that came out instead were a simple, "Thank you."

His body stilled.

I hurriedly added, "You've been selfless since the moment we met, Namir. Focused on protecting me. Helping me heal and grow, too. I'm sure it wasn't easy for you to let me float around the city trying a bunch of random trade work when you knew your brother could use me to kill you."

He remained still, as if my words held him frozen.

I wasn't great at being kind, or sweet. Survival had been my only focus for so long, and I'd just never been inclined to softness like Vena had been. While some people crumbled, or hid, or grew stronger, I hardened.

But with Namir, I couldn't always be that way. I had to be my honest, truthful self.

"You're right; knowing that I was my own monster any earlier would've killed me. I was fighting so hard not to break, back then. And you protected me, even if I don't necessarily like that you had to. That gave me the freedom to live, and evolve. And I know it couldn't have been easy for you to try to figure things out for the both of us with the memories of your mom and dad's shitty relationship bouncing around in your head, so, thank you."

There was another pause.

A long, long pause.

I finally got up the nerve to add, quietly, "I think I might love you for it."

He spun to face me. His eyes were molten, his expression one of fierce need for a split second—and then he crashed into me. His hands were wet and hot on my face as he pinned me to the wall, his lips taking mine in an instant.

My body arched against his, my hands wrapping around the tensed muscles on his biceps as he kissed the hell out of me. His tongue was harsh and brutal, but in a way that exhilarated me.

My grip on him tightened as his hands found my bare thighs, shoving my dress away so he could lift me by my legs. His body held mine against the wall as my feet left the floor, my core meeting his erection in a way that made me groan. The clothes between us were too much—too thick, and definitely in the way. But with our bodies pressed together, both of us wet now, getting the fabric off wouldn't be easy.

And all I wanted to do was keep touching Namir—keep kissing him.

His fingers were nearly on my ass, kneading my flesh and sliding closer to my core. I wanted more—I wanted him.

Ripping my mouth away from his, I snarled at him, "Undress me."

His eyes burned into mine for a moment before I grabbed his face and dragged his mouth back to mine. He made quick work of my dress, and ended up ripping the damned fabric on my underclothing to get it off.

When my nipples met his bare chest, I moaned at the feeling.

His hands were hot on my body—squeezing my ass, tracing my curves, gripping my breasts. I panted as I rocked against his erection, both of us bare and moving together.

The desire to have him fill me was brutal. It was a need—a fierce, hot need that made me think I'd combust if I didn't have it.

I snarled at him again, "I want you inside me."

He growled back, "If we do that, the bond forms. Pregnancy is likely."

I didn't care.

Fate had connected us; Namir was mine—and I wanted him to be mine permanently, regardless of the consequences. Pregnancy was nearly two years for fae, and that was plenty of time for us to cement our bond and get to know each other better.

I didn't know who exactly I wanted to be, or what I wanted to do with my life, but I knew that I wanted Namir with me. And having a baby sure as fuck wouldn't prevent me from being whoever and whatever I wanted. More love was always, always a good thing—and I knew that I would love any child I grew with every ounce of ferocity in my bones.

And those damned bones held a fuck-ton of ferocity.

"*Now*, Namir. I want you inside me *now*."

He parted my thighs further, aligning his erection with my opening. The pressure of his tip against me there was intense, but he wasn't in a hurry—and I wanted him to be in a hurry.

"Don't be gentle. It'll hurt at first, so just get it over with," I commanded.

He growled at me as he thrust himself inside me, not nearly as fast as I wanted him to. He was still being gentle—still protecting me.

And something told me he always would.

…Though I was certain that I could get him to fuck me harder when he knew he wouldn't cause me pain by doing so.

We groaned together as he slid into me, and my body tensed as he broke through whatever strange barrier inside me my body had somehow managed to keep intact despite years of torture.

His eyes burned into mine as he stopped moving for a moment, his erection buried inside me. My chest rose and fell rapidly, matching his heaving one.

He didn't ask if I was okay, but I knew he wouldn't continue until I'd said whether I was or not. Of that, I had no doubt.

"Give me a second," I managed, my eyes closing as my body adjusted to the thickness of him. The sensation was a strange, full one, but a heady one that I loved. "Fuck, Namir."

"That better be a good *fuck*, Love," he growled back, his hands squeezing my ass.

"It is."

"Good. Now open those gorgeous eyes; I want you to look at me while I make love to you."

The sexy command made me groan. "Stars, Namir," I panted, as he thrust back inside me, quickly but not too quickly.

"You feel like fucking heaven, Love," he growled back.

Pressure built inside me rapidly at the intense way he filled me and the hot warmth of feeling him inside my body. My breathing grew shallower as I neared the edge, uncontrollable cries escaping me as he continued pumping in and out of me, not too quickly and not too slowly.

"Lose it with me," I commanded him breathlessly.

"Planning on it," he growled back, his voice rough and hot.

He picked up the pace, moving faster and harder, and my pleasure finally shattered.

I cried out loudly as bliss ripped through me from my head to my toes. Namir snarled as he thrust, his erection throbbing inside me as he soaked me with his own pleasure.

Something within us seemed to snap into place, and a scream tore through me as pleasurable power erupted between us. The air flooded with shadows, energy and strength seeming to rush back into me even as an orgasm rocked every inch of my body.

Emotions flickered through me as I came down from the high again—pleasure, bliss, lust, awe.

Love.

Enough love to make my throat swell, and my eyes water.

I closed them, to make sure that the tears didn't escape.

I wasn't a crier. Not even in my worst, most painful moments, had I given my torturers my tears.

But the wetness in my eyes at the rush of emotions in my heart and mind was unmistakable... and for the first time in my life, I was grateful for them.

CHAPTER 26

THE EMOTIONS FADED AFTER A MOMENT, leaving me shocked and confused. But also, relaxed and feeling *whole* in a way I'd never experienced before.

"Holy shit," I panted, my forehead falling to rest on Namir's shoulder. It was bare, and still wet from the shower raining down on him. I'd been spared from the actual flow of the water, but was still drenched thanks to the king and his body.

"That was fucking incredible, Love," he growled, one of his hands cupping my head as he tugged his forehead back to mine, so they could rest against one another.

"What was that, at the end?" I whispered. "The bond, snapping into place?"

"Yes, the bond snapping into place and our magic weaving together." His lips brushed my cheek. "Thank you, Diora."

"If this is where you tell me you've been using me this whole time, I will fucking kill you even if it takes me out too," I breathed.

He grinned. "Not a damned chance. You're mine, now." His hands slid over my arms, over my sides, over as much of my skin as he could touch in the position we were in. "The throne's power is woven with yours too, now. You'll be faster and stronger, and your healing will be more rapid. One person can't hold both types of magic, but because we each hold one, they can connect the way we can."

"I still can't believe you didn't tell me about that earlier," I growled at him, though the growl was half-hearted with all the pleasure still relaxing my body.

"No more secrets." He eased away from me slightly, his cock still hard and inside me.

"Wait." I grabbed his shoulder, and he paused.

His gaze was calm, steady, and trusting as he waited for me to explain.

Self-consciousness had me biting my lip. "Never mind."

His eyes narrowed at me. "No more secrets, Diora."

I huffed a bit at having the rules turned against me. "I just want you to stay inside me a bit longer. It's stupid."

The narrowness of his eyes was replaced with another grin. "That's not stupid at all. I'll stay inside you for the next week, if you'd like. It's no hardship for me—pun intended."

I snorted. "Terrible pun."

"You loved it." He slipped an arm between my lower back and the wall, hoisting me up a bit before he carried us both backward and into the stream of falling water.

The change of position of him inside me was strange, intense, and... well, incredible.

I bit back a groan as his body flexed a bit, his unoccupied arm stretching back to grab his bar of soap. He dragged it over his arms and head, followed by his neck and shoulders, before tossing it back into place and tugging me closer, his eyes closing as the shower washed the suds away.

"That's hardly cleaning yourself," I remarked, my lower belly still tense with the desire that had already begun to return.

"I'll do better after I've taken you to bed and fucked you again," he said, his lips curving upward in a wicked smirk even as his eyes remained closed.

"Bold of you to assume I'm going to bed with you," I drawled.

His smirk grew more wicked. "You told me I'm too selfless, so this is me asserting myself. You're coming to bed with me, here, every night, and I'll be moving your things into my rooms—we're not fucking around with two bedrooms

anymore, or two sets of clothing. We'll be living together, as
mates should—and making love every morning and night.
Maybe a few times during the day, too."

My lower belly clenched, and Namir throbbed inside me.

"Feels like you like that idea, Love," he remarked, his hands
sliding back down to my backside and giving it a squeeze.

"Bastard," I grumbled.

A low chuckle escaped him. "And the next time you want
your hair done, it'll be my fingers buried in those silky
strands, not Lav's. You belong to me, Diora. No one else.
And as I've said, I don't share."

I scowled, but my lower belly clenched again, and he
throbbed again as I tightened around him. "You're really
taking this and running with it, aren't you?"

He squeezed my ass again. "Hell yes, I am." His hand slid
lower, his fingers running over the sticky, wet place our
bodies connected. I shuddered as he dragged them over the
connection, playing lightly with my hot, sensitive skin, and
the base of his cock where it was buried inside me. "And you
might not admit it, but I think you like it when I take
control."

"For whatever insane reason, I do," I grumbled.

"The reasoning isn't insane. You wanted freedom—what
could be more freeing than surrendering control to the man
fate declared yours, and letting him bring you pleasure

however he wants?" His fingers continued teasing and tracing our connection.

"Bringing myself pleasure?" I shot back, though my breathing was already picking up again.

He gave a rumbly chuckle. "That would come with pressure to make yourself orgasm. With me in charge, you're off the hook for everything, along for the ride. That's true freedom, isn't it?"

I made a noncommittal noise as he shut off the water with one hand, sliding his fingers back around to my ass to hold me up. Namir stepped out of the shower and grabbed a towel for us, wrapping it around me instead of him, and then carried me to the bed without so much as a pause to dry either of us off.

"We're going to soak your bed," I warned.

"Our bed," he corrected me, with a playful grin. "And yes we will—in more ways than one."

My face flushed at the words—and damn, my body reacted.

"Fuck, I love feeling you tighten around me like that. You're even better than I ever imagined, Love." His hands slid smoothly over my back. "I can't wait to taste myself on your lips."

On my...

Ohh.

Shit.

My body clenched again, and his eyes lit up further.

My back met the bed, then, and the breath rushed out of me as I found myself staring up at Namir's throat.

There, on the side of his neck, was the beginning of a mate bond. The first of the letters in the forgotten language, or maybe the first of the words, written on his skin in shimmering gold.

My fingers lifted to the markings, and Namir swore as they brushed the skin. He throbbed inside me a few more times, one of his hands reaching up to hold my fingers still on his skin.

"Careful, Love." His voice was rumbly. "The mark is practically a sexual trigger for your use only."

Damn, I loved the sound of that.

"It won't respond to your touch?" I asked.

He removed my hand from his neck, and rubbed his own fingers over the foreign word without any kind of a reaction.

I batted his away, and dragged mine slowly over the letters.

Namir barked out a curse, seeming to lose control of himself as he slammed himself into me once, twice, and a third time, his erection throbbing as he lost control.

"Dammit, Love," he panted, staring down at me with intensely-shadowed eyes.

A laugh burst from me. "Is it really that—" his thumb dragged over the side of my throat, and a scream escaped me as I bucked my hips, pleasure exploding through me.

His finger remained on my neck, completely still as his hot, dark eyes watched me come down from the high with short, rapid breaths.

"Shit," I mumbled.

"The markings will grow less responsive as they stretch over our throats, but that could take months. There's no set time for a bond to settle completely, as far as I know. But the possessiveness and need will grow more intense as the marks on our throats grow, as well."

"Damn." I closed my eyes, still panting. "That was insane."

"When we've been together more, our bodies will become accustomed to each other, and we'll have more control over it," he murmured. "Theoretically."

I cracked an eye open. "Theoretically?"

He shrugged lightly. "There aren't many mated couples, and those that do exist don't share intimate details about their love lives."

Well, that was just *great*.

"So this is all unknown territory." I gestured between us.

"Not all, but most." His fingers lifted carefully off my neck, and slid into my hair as he rolled me to our sides. "Do you still want to train today?"

I grimaced. "I probably should. The next time Laith shows up, I don't want to be useless."

"The next time Laith shows up, he and his magic won't be able to hurt you. Look." Namir's hand slid out of my hair and found my own, his fingers weaving between mine as he lifted our connected hands up where we could both see them.

His shadows slid off his skin and wrapped around our arms and hands. The feeling of them touching me was just as warm and comforting as it had been before—but there was another level to it.

It felt... like me.

And when I watched closely, I could see and feel my own shadows twisted with his, our different magics dancing and swirling together.

"You're stronger than both your brothers, now," I whispered to him.

Neither of them had their personal magic back, but since we were bonded, he could apparently access his through me.

"And yet my desire to end their lives is smaller than it's ever been before," he admitted, his voice soft. "I want a life with you Diora. Not a throne, or a war, or a field of dead fae. A peaceful, happy life."

"That's what would make you a good king, though," I murmured.

He sighed heavily. "Don't speak reason to me when I'm buried inside you, woman."

The joke fell flat, but my lips still curved upward sadly. "I wish there was an easy way out of this mess with your brothers too, Namir."

He went silent for a moment.

My eyes narrowed a bit. "Is there?"

"Now that we're mated, I could surrender the throne magic to one of them. It would be a simple ending to our fight, but not necessarily the right thing to do. Things are complex."

"Complex how?" I asked.

He slowly slid himself out from within me, rolling to his back and collapsing to the bed. I sprawled half my body over his, propping myself up on one arm so I could see him better as he spoke.

"I told you about my parents; my mother's cruelty, and my father's unwillingness to stop her. Despite that, they constantly disagreed on which of us should rule after them— which was why the throne's magic was divided after their deaths in the first place."

I nodded, my curiosity growing.

"You've met Laith. He's not a good man, but he was the only one of us my mother liked in the slightest. He's the second oldest, and she was determined that he was the one who should take the throne. I told you about Espen—he's the oldest, and the one my father was always vocal about giving the power to. But Espen never wanted it, and he never protected himself when our mother would lose her temper. He's much older now, and has defended his part of the court from Laith for decades, but I can't say I trust him enough to just hand him the magic. And obviously, I can't give it to Laith."

I grimaced. "You're right; it's not an easy situation."

He nodded, and was quiet for a few minutes. His fingers played with my wet braid, and my thoughts turned a bit.

"Espen has the moon's magic, right? He's the Night King?" I checked.

Namir dipped his chin in a nod.

"Akari holds his magic. I wonder if they're connected, like we are."

His expression turned thoughtful. "I've wondered the same. Honestly, you possessing my magic is probably what pushed fate to create the connection between us. It would surprise me tremendously if she held his magic, yet he was fated to be with someone else."

I had been thinking the same thing.

"Of my friends, Akari was the only one of us who was really after revenge," I said quietly. "Your people murdered her family when they wouldn't hand her over without a fight; there weren't many weak fae who could survive taking someone else's magic."

Namir's expression darkened. "Stars."

"I know. She's... well, she won't give up as easily as I did, when it comes to killing your brother."

"He'll have her in his dungeon, then. He's undoubtedly changed, but he's enough like my father in that way." Namir's fingers continued playing with my braid, tugging gently at the strands. "If we ever want to end this war, I'll have to talk to Espen in person. I haven't seen him in two decades, but one of us will have to give our magic to the other if we're going to defeat Laith."

"Then it sounds like we need to take a journey," I murmured.

He nodded, his expression darkening. "I'm hesitant to leave my people without protection."

"Most of your warriors have strong magic, they just don't know how to access it. I can teach them, and Lavee can as well, now that she's figured it out."

"I'd still like to know what you taught her," he remarked.

I flashed him a smile. "You can sit in on one of my lessons."

His eyes softened, his fingers lifting to brush my lips. "I love that smile."

I pressed a light kiss to his fingertips. "It's here because of you."

"Why do you think I like it so much?" His tease was gentle, but I laughed anyway.

"I'm glad I didn't kill you."

"As am I, Love." He winked at me, lifting his lips to kiss my cheek.

CHAPTER 27

WE MADE love a few more times before we finally cleaned up and slipped out of Namir's room.

Our room.

Though, how long it belonged to us was up in the air considering we would need to leave soon, so we could make our way to Espen's part of the court. It would be a three-month journey just to get to his castle, so it was important for us to leave as soon as possible.

Especially since I might find myself growing a baby in the coming weeks or months, and Namir would probably get more possessive and difficult when that happened.

When we made it to the training room, we found Lavee already talking to the warriors about magic, so Namir and I leaned up against the room's doorway instead of going in.

My braid was draped over the marking on my neck, and Namir's was probably hidden by my head or shoulder, so the change in our relationship wasn't immediately obvious to anyone around us.

Lavee didn't teach them about using it like a hand, or making it work with you, but about finding it. Feeling it, in your chest. Locating that spark of power, the wildness in your middle, and embracing it.

She flashed me a curious look when her instructions paused to let people practice for a moment, and though she didn't ask aloud, I was pretty sure she was checking to make sure I was okay with her teaching the warriors instead of me. I gave her a quick smile back, and she relaxed.

And honestly, I was glad I didn't have to train them myself. If she knew how to explain it, she could take that job permanently. I wasn't sure exactly what I wanted to do with my life, but I wasn't considering the role of magic teacher. Patience wasn't one of my virtues, so teaching was not the job for me.

Namir's arms were around my body, holding my back to his chest while the lesson went on. He didn't say anything to me, but our shadows danced slowly around us.

It felt incredible, honestly. And not in a sexual way—in a comfortable, easy, peaceful way.

A happy way, even.

"Thinking about me?" Namir murmured, his lips only a breath from my ear.

"No," I lied.

He chuckled, his teeth scraping my earlobe. "I love it when you lie to me."

My lips curved upward, just the tiniest bit.

"You felt our emotions collide after the bond fell into place, right?" His voice was still soft, quiet enough that no one nearby would hear.

"Mmhm."

"We'll be able to communicate mentally at some point. I don't know when exactly, but soon, I hope."

I didn't want to admit it, but I hoped so too.

Being able to communicate mentally would give us a way to converse more easily... and would make it much harder for us to have misunderstandings, I thought.

We watched the lesson until Lavee had everyone start practicing their magic. Then, Namir scooped me up into his arms and strode into the room.

I scowled up at him, earning a playful wink, and assumed he was heading toward the throne he had unceremoniously shoved into the corner of the room. Instead, he walked over to the few stairs leading up toward it, and then sat down. He set me on my ass on the stair below the one he occupied, holding my back to his chest with his arms around me loosely, but firmly as well.

We were getting a lot of curious looks, but Lavee growled at anyone who wasn't practicing with their magic, so eventually they got over the strangeness of seeing us like that and focused on what they were doing.

Namir's shadows slid around us, and I could feel his magic shifting and stretching as he tested the instructions Lav had given. While I didn't know if it was helping him use more of his power—our power, now that our magic was bound—the feeling of it sliding over my skin and filling the air around me was a bit surreal. Warm, and comfortable, and right.

I felt settled in a way I hadn't known I could.

I felt... at home.

Not in the castle, but with Namir. With our magic in the air, and our bodies touching. Not sexually, but intimately nonetheless.

The room exploded with moonlight as the first of the fae warriors found her magic. Cheers and whoops went through the room as the light dissipated, and I saw the female fae grinning and slapping hands with the people around her.

She continued practicing her magic with the others, and one by one, more warriors found the triggers to their magic.

Some of the magical bursts were much smaller than others, and some of the warriors had already discovered how to tune into their magic on their own, but didn't possess the same level of power as the fae whose magic practically exploded.

Namir murmured sexy words and stupid jokes into my ear every now and then, his magic continuously floating around us and filling the air we occupied. Time passed quickly, and I felt happy.

Really happy.

Over time the warriors trickled out to celebrate and practice their magic on their own, until there were only six of us left in the room—me and Namir, Jesh, Lavee, and two other male fae I sort of recognized.

Lavee stood on the opposite side of the room from Jesh, talking animatedly with the other two male fae. Jesh's eyes were narrowed, his body tensed as he went through some type of routine with his sword that included some strange stretches, turns, and slashes. He was pointedly not looking at Lavee, but Namir and I had noticed that he hadn't figured out how to tap into his magic.

My gaze lingered on him, and Namir nipped at my earlobe for probably the fiftieth time since we'd been sitting in the training room.

"Watch your eyes, Love. I don't want to kill anyone," he murmured playfully.

"He looks angry," I murmured back.

"Any man refusing to acknowledge feelings for his fated mate would be."

My eyebrows shot upward.

He had feelings for Lavee?

My gaze slid over to her; she was grinning as she talked with the other fae men.

"Want to help me get him to acknowledge those emotions?" I checked quietly.

"I've tried. He's a stone wall." Namir nipped at my ear again.

"Just play along," I told him, standing smoothly.

The king reluctantly rose with me, and his arms left my body as he captured my hand, threading his fingers between mine. He let me take the lead, remaining beside me as I crossed the room, headed over to Jesh.

Jesh congratulated us on the development of our bond, now that he could see the markings on our necks, but his voice was stiff.

"Need help?" I asked him, gesturing to the sword in his hand that most definitely wasn't drenched in moonlight.

He scowled my way. "How did you help Lav?"

"I can show you, but you've got to stop glaring at me. My king here doesn't take well to threats." I tilted my head toward Namir, and he flashed Jesh a wicked grin.

"You know it's true, brother."

Jesh scowled. "Fine."

I shaped the shadows Namir had around us into a sphere, like I had done with Lavee in the forest, and used them to separate us from the rest of the room.

"If you want my help, you don't protest my methods. Do what I say, when I say it, and don't complain," I said sharply.

His scowl deepened, but he jerked his head in a nod.

He was in a shitty mood of the likes I'd rarely seen from him —and I was almost positive that Lavee was to blame for it.

And I was going to use that.

"Close your eyes," I told him.

He did, though I was fairly confident he would've growled at me for the command if Namir hadn't already threatened him.

"Picture yourself back in the training room," I instructed.

Namir's arms wrapped around me again, and he stepped up to me until his chest was to my back once more.

"Not with your magic, but with your swords. You're practicing with Namir, while Lavee talks to a man in the corner." I mentally scrambled for a name of one of the more attractive male fae warriors I'd met. "She laughs with Kaiz, and your foot slips. Namir takes the opportunity to disarm you, and his sword lands against your throat just as you hear Lavee agree to go dancing with Kaiz tonight."

Jesh's scowl deepened. "She hasn't been out with any men since we realized our connection."

Maybe that was part of the problem.

"Shut up and listen," I growled back.

He shut up, though he looked annoyed about doing so.

"Lav slips out of the room a bit later, and you don't say anything as she leaves, even though you're tempted to ask her about it. You listen closely for the sounds of her coming home all night, and when you don't hear them, you don't go to sleep. You end up in the hallway as morning approaches, pacing in front of her door. She finally reaches the top of the staircase, her braid undone and her hair tangled, her face happier than you've ever seen it, and her body reeking of another man's pleasure. You—"

A snarl escaped Jesh, and moonlight flickered off his skin. "Enough."

"Watch your tone." Namir's voice was no longer playful.

"It's alright. If he doesn't want my help, he doesn't have to take it," I drawled, stepping away from Jesh as if I hadn't expected that to happen.

Namir was probably a bit confused, but his confident façade remained as I dropped the shadowed sphere from around us.

"I can take a stab at it," Namir said casually, releasing my waist.

I could've kissed him for realizing what I was doing—or at least giving me space to do it.

"Fine," Jesh growled at us. His voice was slightly less angry, but I shot him a glare before I stepped away anyway.

Lavee eyed me curiously, as I headed back to the place Namir and I had sat on the stairs for a while. When I slyly gestured her toward me, she excused herself from the conversation with the men she'd been helping and crossed the room. After plopping down beside me unceremoniously, she murmured, "What was that about?"

"Helping Jesh with his magic and pulling his head out of his ass at the same time," I murmured back.

She lifted an eyebrow at me. "How?"

"What's the one thing you can't help but feel toward your fated mate, Lav?"

Her eyes narrowed. "Possessive."

"Mmhm. I tried to teach him the same way I taught you—now, you just need to convince someone to act like they're fucking you."

Lav grimaced. "You're an evil mastermind now?"

"I'm a brilliant friend now," I corrected. Lowering my voice, I added, "You see the mark on my neck. I felt the bond snap into place between me and Namir, and you deserve to have that too. It's incredible, Lav. If all it takes is a fake date or two with a friend, isn't it worth it?"

She heaved a sigh. "I hate you for being right."

"You'll love me for it eventually." I leaned back, spreading my hands on the stairs. "I set the bait, now you get to decide whether or not to dangle the stick."

She snorted. "That's terrible."

"I know." I flashed her a grin.

She heaved a sigh, then stood up. "Wish me luck."

"You won't need it."

I watched her cross the room, headed back to the men practicing their magic. Jesh's narrowed eyes followed her, and she must've noticed it, because she started off with adding more instructions to the guys.

When Jesh and Namir were fighting with their magic, Namir keeping his shadows toned down, Lavee stepped closer to the men and murmured a few quick words.

I saw grins on their faces, along with nods of agreement, and then they returned to practicing.

Everyone continued for a bit longer, until one of the men remarked, "Clearly, I'm a lost cause. I think I'm going to celebrate my failure with a night of wine and sex. Either of you want in?" He winked at them.

I bit back a snort.

Sly.

So sly.

"Eh, I just want to sleep." The second guy shrugged. "Maybe next time."

Both men looked at Lavee.

I noticed Jesh had called for a break in the fighting, and was sipping from a water bottle with his hand clenched around the thing so damn tightly I wondered if it would break.

Lavee hesitated.

"Come on." The wine-and-sex guy nudged her with his elbow, grinning more widely at her. "I'll buy. You've got even more of a reason to celebrate than I do, and we all know it's been ages since you've had a good time."

Lavee sighed. "Persuasive bastard. Fine, I'm in. I'll need backup, though. Diora?" She shot a grin my way. "Have you ever even tried wine?"

She had surprised me, but I could play along.

I shrugged. "No."

"Come on, it'll be fun. And considering the mark on your neck, it's probably your last chance to try drinking for the next two years."

I felt Namir's eyes on me, but didn't look his way. We were mates, and I cared about his comfort, but he still needed to trust me.

And... I wanted to go. To experience the wine-drinking and whatnot. There would be no sex for me until I got back to the castle, obviously, but I could still enjoy myself. "Alright, fine."

I finally looked at Namir, and found him wearing a genuine, playful grin. He approved of me going, and was still okay with being away from me for short periods of time; that was good. "Come find me in a few hours, *Love*?" My voice took on the teasing tone it always had when I attempted to use his accent and his nickname against him.

His grin widened. "You'll be lucky if I last two without you. Don't worry though; I'll bring chocolate to lure your sexy, drunk ass back to my bed."

I snorted. "Good call."

"It's settled," the wine-and-sex guy declared, looping his arm through Lav's. I stepped toward them, but Namir beat me there. He'd crossed the room in two steps, stopping in front of the guy whose name I still didn't know.

His voice lowered, his eyes narrowing at the male fae. "If another man so much as touches one hair on my female's arm, I will hold you personally responsible."

The guy's expression grew just as serious as Namir's. "If another man so much as stares at the queen, I'll take his head off."

Namir's head dipped in a nod, and he stepped to the side, gesturing toward the door. His lips lifted in one of his genuine, playful grins as he snagged my hand and used it to tug me to his chest. His hand wrapped around the back of my neck, and our lips crashed into each other for a moment. The kiss was brutal, and possessive, and claiming, and I returned it just as enthusiastically as he gave it.

When he finally pulled away, he murmured against my lips, "You're mine, Love. Best not forget that for both of our sakes."

Goosebumps went up my spine. "I won't." I dragged my teeth over his lower lip, releasing it as I stepped back. "Watch yourself while I'm gone, Namir," I called back as I strode over to a grinning Lavee and the guy whose name I still didn't know. We slipped out the door, and I added without turning around, "If I get a report of any flirting, I'll do far worse than take a few heads off."

My king's booming laugh had me fighting a grin as we walked away.

CHAPTER 28

WE MADE our way through the city, grinning about the possibility of Jesh finally being forced to realize that Lavee was the perfect woman for him. I learned the male fae's name —Ander—and we chatted about how the magic lessons had gone during the day.

It was lighthearted, and fun, and I found myself laughing far more than I expected.

We walked into the bar, and I looked around curiously. Though I'd been to a lot of places in the city, I'd never made it there before.

The building was large, with most of the ceiling open to the sky above, and the walls lined with slim tables and stools. In two opposite corners of the room, the tables were angled so there was a triangular gap between them and the wall, with plenty of space for a bartender to mix, pour, and serve drinks.

Relaxed but upbeat music came from a few instruments I didn't have names for, and when Lavee noticed me staring at the musicians on a short stage in the center of the building, she murmured the names of the instruments to me.

Between the stools and the stage, there were large, bare stretches of space. In those spaces, couples moved and danced and spun, some with feet moving rapidly and others merely swaying slowly around the dance floor, lost in either the alcohol or the buzz of each others' arms.

We got our first drinks from one of the bartenders—Lavee had some kind of mixed cocktail, but told me to start with the wine since I was a newbie. I trusted her, and sipped at the drink she got me. It was somehow both sweet and bitter at the same time, but she grinned and told me I'd get used to it when she saw me make a face at the taste.

Ander picked some strange moonshine, and Lavee told me I'd better not touch that shit or Namir was going to kill her.

Of course, that nearly made me curious enough to get a glass of it myself. But, I figured I'd better wait and see how the wine affected me first.

A few people I didn't recognize came over to chat with Lavee and Ander, making an effort to include me in the conversation too. I didn't say much, though, not knowing most of what they were talking about. But it was still nice to be out, among other people. And I loved watching the other fae dance. I wasn't good at it—not in the slightest—but I'd enjoyed dancing when I did it. The way my body moved across the floor, the way the music seemed to make my shadows sway and spin with me... there was something beautiful about it.

I was going to learn how to fight—there didn't seem to be a way around that. But, I decided, if I was going to learn how to fight, I needed to learn something beautiful too. Something creative, and useful, and free. I didn't want my life to be empty again when the fighting with Namir's brothers was over. I still wanted to *live*.

I wasn't a prisoner anymore; I was free, and safe.

And happy.

Outrageously, ridiculously happy.

My eyes followed the fae on the dance floor while I continued sipping at my drink. Lavee was right; it got easier to drink the longer I worked on it.

Time passed, and my body warmed and relaxed.

I was starting to understand why people liked drinking.

The urge to hit the dance floor flooded me, and I nudged Lavee with an arm. "Let's go dance."

She lifted an eyebrow at me. "You think I can dance?"

"I know you can fight, so yes, I think you can dance." My voice sounded a bit funny, but I slid off my stool and tugged her toward the floor. She laughed, cutting off her conversation with the random people she'd been talking to. Her hand caught on Ander's arm, and she tugged him out with us. There were a few other guys with him, and they all watched Lavee move, paying little attention to me.

Maybe some women would've hated that, but I loved it. Knowing that she was the one they were staring at gave me freedom to be a shitty dancer, freedom to spin and shake my ass and do whatever the hell I wanted.

Maybe it wasn't just Lavee who freed me from their attention though—maybe it was the marking on my neck that connected me to Namir, designating me as taken.

Lavee ignored the men watching her, stepping up close to me as we shimmied and shook, moving with the music and shaking our hips with the rhythm. It was fast and upbeat, dragging grins onto our faces as we danced our asses off.

More time passed, and Lavee was lured into the group of men while I grinned from the other side of the group, dancing on my own with flushed cheeks and a heady, blissed-out feeling relaxing me.

I hoped Lavee and Jesh would figure things out, but if they didn't... well, I wanted her to be happy anyway. She had wanted love since they met, and he had turned her down. So I wanted that for her—I wanted her to have the relationship she wanted, the future she wanted.

There was no guarantee that Jesh would be waiting outside her door to claim her and snarl at her when we got back that night.

There was no guarantee that he would ever even admit that he wanted her.

But she still deserved her happiness, so I was glad to see her grinning and laughing as she danced up against a couple of the other fae warriors she seemed to know well.

A few minutes later, a set of arms wrapped around my waist, a chiseled chest meeting my back. Had our shadows not wrapped around me a moment before his arms did, I would've panicked. But the feel of our connected magic had calmed me and warned me, so I wasn't surprised or uncomfortable in the slightest.

"Keep moving, Love. Dance with me," Namir murmured into my ear, his hands on my hips. My ass was pressed to his erection, our bodies swaying as one. It was comfortable but thrilling at the same time, somehow.

"Jesh followed me here. I might have to let go of you to grab him if a fight breaks out," he warned, his lips still against my ear and his voice soft and light. "I've never seen him like that. He was losing his damned mind. He and Lav agreed not to fuck anyone else when they found out what they were to each other—I guess maybe this was the only trigger he's needed since the beginning."

"We can protect everyone else here if we need to," I murmured back.

"Mmhm." He dragged his teeth over my earlobe. "Stars, you smell good. How drunk are you?"

I snorted. "Hard to say."

He chuckled, but before he could speak a response, a snarl tore through the room.

Moonlight brightened the space off to my side, and my head tilted as I turned to see the source.

Light flickered off Jesh's skin as he stalked across the room, his sword clenched in one hand and his other formed into a fist.

The music stopped, and I saw shadows engulf the musicians for a moment as they slipped away from the upcoming drama. My king had their back, as he always seemed to when it came to his people.

"Damn," I remarked, speaking both about Jesh and the easy way my man had shielded the musicians. My mind was still a bit clouded, but not clouded enough to prevent me from noticing the smooth way he reacted to the danger.

"If you're checking him out, I'll kill him," Namir whispered into my ear, making me snort.

My king was possessive, but not *that* possessive.

When he turned his head to meet my cheek, I felt his grin against the side of my face, too, confirming my suspicions.

"Get your fucking hands off my mate," Jesh snarled at the group of men, who were still circling Lavee—but now facing her pissed-off male. None of them were touching her any longer, but they didn't make any move to step away.

I saw most of the men's eyes flicker toward Namir and I before anyone reacted. I didn't know whether they were checking to see if they needed to protect me, or to see whether or not Namir and I were there to protect *them* if necessary, but I didn't really care.

"Last I checked, you hadn't claimed her," Ander remarked, slipping an arm over Lav's shoulder as if it was the most natural thing in the world.

More moonlight flickered off Jesh, light covering more of his body and flashing brighter by the second. "Tell them before I kill someone, Lav."

She lifted an eyebrow. "Tell them what, exactly? That you don't want me physically, and never have?"

Jesh's light flickered brighter, and hotter. There was fury in his voice as he snarled back, "I have *always* wanted you."

She lifted an eyebrow. "Right."

He stalked toward her, his light growing brighter and bigger by the moment. "Back away," he commanded the men.

They glanced over at Namir and I again, so quickly that I wouldn't have caught it if I hadn't been standing where I was.

I felt Namir give a small, quick nod, his cheek to mine though he still stood behind me, his arms wrapped around my front.

All of the men parted, giving Jesh and Lavee space—except Ander, who didn't move.

There was a wicked gleam in that bastard's eyes, and I knew he was going to play this out until the end. That made me like the guy even more than I had before.

"You. Are. Mine." Jesh's voice came out low and gravelly, and the heat in the room seemed to rise despite none of us having the elemental magic that other lands around us possessed.

"Prove it," Lavee shot back.

Ander's arm finally left her shoulder as Jesh's magic exploded. Light flooded the room, but our shadows wrapped protectively around everyone else in the building, shielding all of us from the full extent of Jesh's power. Namir's hips continued swaying with mine just a bit, and my eyes closed as my body soaked in the intoxicating bliss brought on by both the alcohol I'd consumed and the feel of our combined magic surrounding me so thickly.

The shadows faded as Jesh's light did as well, and when both types of night magic cleared enough for us to see in the room, my eyes widened as they caught on Jesh and Lavee.

He had her pinned to the wall, her arms above her head as he kissed her brutally.

"You're taking me to bed, or I'm going to fucking kill you," Lav snarled at him, as she pulled away for the briefest moment.

His teeth skimmed her throat, and he growled back, "I'm not letting you out of my bed for the next fucking *year*, Lav."

And then their mouths found each other again, the moonlight and all-consuming darkness clashing together as their bodies did the same.

"Should we tell them to find a room?" I asked, fighting a grin.

"They'll leave before they get to the good parts," Namir said, his tongue, lips, and teeth moving slowly over the side of my neck. He added, "I hope."

A laugh bubbled out of me.

Stars, the alcohol was strong.

"What now?" I asked Namir.

"Now, everyone goes back to whatever they were doing before Jesh stormed in." His hips were still swaying with mine, and I wasn't sure which of us was responsible for the movement.

"And us?"

"We dance until you're sober enough to go back to our rooms and fuck me." He nipped at my shoulder, making me laugh again.

"I'm not a great dancer."

"I'm good enough for both of us," he teased, earning another laugh from me.

We continued swaying as the musicians made their way back to their stage. My eyes kept drifting to Jesh and Lavee, but their magic made their forms too hazy to really see what was going on.

The music began again, and Jesh finally hauled Lavee out of the bar, holding her with her legs around his hips.

"Shall we dance for real, Love?" my king drawled, spinning me so my arms wrapped around his shoulders. Another laugh escaped me, and I tilted my head back a bit as he pulled me closer, one of his hands capturing mine and the other sliding up my back as he got into position.

"We shall," I drawled back, earning a grin.

Namir whisked me around the dance floor like it was the most important thing in the world—and for the next few hours, it felt like it was.

CHAPTER 29

WHEN WE FINALLY MADE IT back to our room, we crashed together so hard and fast that we didn't even take our clothes off.

I supposed I might owe Lavee some gold for that, but considering all that had happened that night, I was pretty sure she'd waive the bet.

I dreamed about being chained up in the prison I'd spent so much of my life in that night, and when I woke up panicking and shaking, Namir held me and murmured sweet words to me until I was calm enough to fall back into a dreamless sleep.

I'd never dreamed before I met Namir—the kings of sleep seemed to have given me a pass when it came to dreaming before then. But now that I had a mate, and a home, and more people who loved me, I supposed they had decided that I was ready to have dreams and nightmares as well.

The next morning, we woke up with another set of markings on our throats. My head ached a little, but Namir assured me that the hangover would fade quickly thanks to the throne's magic.

WE SPENT the next few days training and preparing the warriors to defend the city without Namir's assistance, still spending our evenings practicing my reading and writing, of course.

Jesh and Lavee remained absent, but no one had dared try to interrupt them. They were Namir's closest friends in the court, but they weren't the top guards, so that wasn't a huge problem.

When a week had gone by, we decided it was time to leave. There was nothing to be gained by waiting any longer, and Namir was anxious to talk to Espen and hopefully begin working their way toward peace.

Rather than making a spectacle of leaving, we slipped out of the castle before anyone else woke up, heading out with our fingers intertwined and our shoulders brushing as we walked.

A few hours down the road, two figures caught up to us. I glanced over, and did a double-take when I saw the massive man with his huge-ass braid, and his grinning redheaded mate at his side. They wore the single marks on their throats proudly, their hands intertwined like mine and Namir's.

"I wondered how long it would take you to catch up," Namir tossed out, flashing them a grin.

"Oh, fuck off," Lav shot back, making me grin.

Even Jesh grinned at her words.

"I didn't know you were coming," I said, glancing up at Namir.

He winked at me. "Didn't want to get your hopes up in case Jesh really survived that year of sex he had planned."

"He couldn't," Lave agreed. "Doesn't have the stamina for —" She cut herself off as she erupted with laughter, her gigantic male tickling her sides in revenge.

"My stamina had nothing to do with it," Jesh growled, though his lips were still curved upward in a half-grin. "Lav's nauseous already. Puked three times last night."

My eyebrows shot upward. "Already pregnant?"

She grinned at me, the expression bigger and brighter than any I'd seen from her. "Yep."

"Shit. How do you know?" I checked.

"You can feel it with your magic." She released Jesh, grabbing my arm. "Here, I'll show you. Turn around, bastards." She waved them off.

Both men turned around, though they grumbled as they did so.

"Why did they need to turn around?" I whispered, as she led me away from them.

She winked at me. "They didn't. I just like to annoy them."

I snorted, and she grinned. "Here."

We stopped just far enough away that I didn't think they'd hear us. There were trees surrounding us, and since we were still in our forests, the shadows danced through the trees, tugging lightly at any loose strands of our hair as the light breeze did the same.

"Put your hand here." She lowered her hand to her heart. "A fae child starts as a tiny flicker of magic, buried in the center of his or her mother's power. If it's there, there'll be no mistaking the feeling."

I nodded, closing my eyes and focusing on my magic. It was still so surreal to feel Namir's power intertwined with mine, the magic breathtakingly-strong yet also soft and comforting.

When I felt that spark—the small, almost nonexistent spark—in the center of my power, my eyes flew open, my lips parting.

It didn't feel like magic, it felt like... life.

"Shit," I breathed.

Lav's grin widened. "Our babies will be best friends," she decided, throwing an arm around my shoulder and walking me back to the men.

"Or worst enemies," I tossed back.

That only made her laugh. "I'll be fine with either."

I would too, to be honest.

"Alright assholes, you can turn back around," Lav declared. Both men spun, and my eyes collided with Namir's.

He wore his usual playful grin, but now I knew how to read his emotions beneath it.

He was nervous—and hopeful.

"I'm pregnant," I admitted.

"Just what the world needs—another Night royal fighting for the throne," Jesh drawled.

Lavee released me so she could stride over and elbow him in the gut, hard.

Namir crossed the space between us in two steps, his hands cupping my face. "Let me feel," he murmured.

I nodded, watching intently as he closed his eyes.

A moment passed, and then his expression shifted to one of wonder. "Stars, Love," he breathed.

"It's a good thing we've got two years to get ready," I admitted, biting my lip.

He swept me off the ground and into his arms, capturing my lips with his. My arms wrapped around his neck as he kissed the hell out of me, our shadows swirling around us.

"You are fucking incredible," he told me, his eyes shining with emotion.

I flashed him a small smile. "You're not so bad yourself."

Our lips collided again, and the kiss continued until Lavee whistled. "Hey, love-buns, we've got to hit the road if we want to make it to an inn before the sun sets. Especially since I'll probably have to stop and vomit a handful of times before then.

Namir and I exchanged grimaces.

"I really hope I don't get morning sickness," I said, as he set me back down on my feet.

"Nothing about this is *morning* related," Lav tossed back.

We exchanged grins, and continued on our way.

THE NEXT FEW months passed by slowly, but quickly too. There was something peaceful about being on the road, and something therapeutic about knowing that all I had to do day after day was continue walking, and chatting, and eating.

Namir and I grew closer day by day, and my friendships with Lavee and Jesh grew stronger as well. It took me a while to finally forgive Jesh for spilling my secret on that first day we met, but I did get over it.

Eventually.

When we finally stopped at an inn just outside Espen's city, I was actually disappointed that our journey was over. Despite my pregnancy (I'd gotten lucky and hadn't puked once, unlike Lavee with her near-constant sickness), I had never felt more peace or happiness in my life.

Namir and I split from Jesh and Lav as we went to our rooms. After he and I showered together, we collapsed into bed, clean, naked, and tired.

His hand roamed my slightly-curved abdomen, as it always seemed to when we stopped for the night. "Is the baby kicking yet?" he murmured, his forehead resting against the side of mine as he stroked my abdomen, reaching up to play with my breasts every minute or two as well.

"No. Lav says it'll be another month or two before we feel kicks, if not three or four," I murmured back, my eyes closing at the blissful comfort of having his hands on me so gently. "I hope I can figure out how to be a mother, when he or she is born," I admitted.

"We'll figure it out together." My king kissed my cheek, and then my lips.

"Are you nervous about seeing Espen tomorrow?" I asked, though we'd already talked about it a handful of times. Namir liked to try to carry the weight of all his worries on his own, so I reminded him often that we were a team—and that I could help him handle things better. We were still learning how to share our burdens, but we were getting better at it by the day.

"Still no," he admitted. "I'm much more worried about your plan to break into his damn dungeon."

My lips curved up in a wicked smile. "It's going to be a blast."

"Not literally, I hope," he teased me, his voice light and playful.

Stars, I loved him.

"Not literally," I agreed, my smile softening into a happy, comfortable expression. "But you think that's where Akari will be, so we have to check to make sure. If he kicks us from his castle after you attempt a peace talk, we don't want to have to break in again."

"I know, Love. I helped you plan it. I just worry about you." His hand slid down my belly, and between my thighs. "I'd better make sure you smell like me before you break into a dungeon with Jesh," he murmured, tilting my head with his other hand as he kissed down the side of my throat. His lips brushed the far edge of the full line of ancient words on my neck, and I gasped as his tongue snaked out, licking the sexual trigger.

A release tore through me, leaving me breathless and moaning, "Dammit, Namir."

He chuckled against my neck, and I could feel that damned playful grin. "That was one point for me, Love." His fingers stroked the bundle of nerves between my thighs, making me pant as he worked on me. He was already rock-hard; he was always hard for me.

And as he parted my legs, sliding his erection inside me, I couldn't help but think how fucking glad I was that I hadn't killed him in his throne room that day. Our lives were far from perfect, but they meant everything to me.

I hadn't known true freedom until I met Namir, and now, I knew without question that I could do anything and be anyone... and that he would love me no matter what.

Epilogue

Namir

"Protect her, but don't touch her," I growled at Jesh, raking my hair into place the way I'd worn it the last time I saw Espen. I wanted him to see his younger brother in me, so he didn't try to kill me on-site if he'd turned into as much of a bastard as Laith had.

"We've been over this a dozen times already," Jesh growled back. "I have no desire to touch your female, and you'd sure as fuck better not touch mine."

Diora and Lavee rolled their eyes at each other—I supposed they were tired of this argument.

"Let's get this show on the road," Lav urged, shooing Jesh and Diora toward the left side of the castle, where I knew the guards' entrance to the prison was located. I'd grown up in Espen's castle, and knew it better than my own even after two decades away from it.

"A kiss for luck, first," I growled, snagging Diora's waist.

"You've already kissed her for luck twice," Jesh grumbled at me.

"Shut up, they're adorable," Lav shot back at her mate, elbowing him in the abdomen to shut him up.

He grunted, but quieted as I captured Diora's lips in my own.

"I'll be fine," Diora promised me, her golden eyes bright and happy.

She had transformed over the last few months, coming to life more day by day as she settled into the knowledge that I loved her, and would always love her—and into the knowledge that she could control her magic, and would never be controlled by it again.

"Just be careful, please," I murmured, my hand sliding over the sexy curve of her belly.

Our small life was growing within her, and I was more paranoid than ever because of it.

But my mate's friend was important to her, so we had to do this—and it was worth the attempt for peace.

"I'll meet you in the throne room," she promised, squeezing my hand before she stepped away. The intricate braids she'd let me weave her hair into kept the strands out of her face and off her shoulders, showing off the curve of that gorgeous neck as she turned.

I shoved away my possessive instinct to whisk her away and lock her in a damned tower or something, both to ensure her safety and keep her as my own. Instead, I glanced at Lavee. "Ready?"

"Yup." She flashed me a grin.

We would get my brother on-board with our peace plan...

Even if we had to use his fated mate to do it.

I prayed to the stars as we strode in like we owned the place that Akari had as much sway over Espen as Diora had over me, because there was a damned good chance we would need her.

THE END

Read Espen and Akari's story in
Imprisoned by the Night King

Afterthoughts

What an exciting ride, huh? Honestly, this book was kind of a doozy, but not for the reasons I expected.

First off, I had SO much fun writing it. Creating this court, with its warring brothers and the survivor women they're paired with was an absolute blast.

But I'll say this—it's been a long time since I've had to edit any book as extensively as I did this one.

Namir was a hard main character to pin down. In the first version, he was moodier, and worse at hiding his emotions, and not what Diora needed.

But as I went back and changed things, he grew more upbeat. More playful. More complex.

Honestly, I didn't even expect him to turn out to be a cheerful guy when I first sat down and wrote this book. I'm always afraid I'll cross the oh-so-slim line between having a nice male love interest and a sexy pansy dude. But Namir's cheerfulness happened, and I'm here for it!

Anyway, I love this book, and I love these characters. I've already started on Espen and Akari's story, and damn, it's going to be blast. I hope to see you at the end of that book, too!

inserts un-sly wink

Thank you so much for reading!

All the love,

Lola Glass

PLEASE REVIEW

Here it is. The awkward page at the end of the book where
the author begs you to leave a review.
Believe me, I hate it more than you do.
But, this is me swallowing my pride and asking.
Whether you loved or hated this story, you made it this far, so
please review! Your reviews play a MASSIVE role in
determining whether others read my books, and ultimately,
writing is a job for me—even if it's the best job ever—so I
write what people are reading.
Regardless of whether you do or not, thank you so much for
reading <3
-Lola

Also by Lola Glass:

Night's Curse Standalones

Burning Kingdom Trilogy

Moon of the Monsters Trilogy

Sacrificed to the Fae King Trilogy

Shifter Queen Trilogy

Rejected Mate Refuge Trilogy

Outcast Pack Standalones

Mate Hunt Standalones

Wolfsbane Series

Shifter City Trilogy

Supernatural Underworld Duology

STOP BY

Check out my reader group, Lola's Book Lovers
for giveaways, book recommendations, and more!

Or find me on:
TIKTOK
INSTAGRAM
PINTEREST
GOODREADS

About the Author

Lola is a book-lover with a *slight* romance obsession and a passion for love—real love. Not the flowers-and-chocolates kind of love, but the kind where two people build a relationship strong enough to last. That's the kind of relationship she loves to read about, and the kind she tries to portray in her books.

Even if they're about shifters :)